Thomas Carlyle, Charles Townsend Copeland

Letters of Thomas Carlyle to his Youngest Sister

Thomas Carlyle, Charles Townsend Copeland

Letters of Thomas Carlyle to his Youngest Sister

ISBN/EAN: 9783337017040

Printed in Europe, USA, Canada, Australia, Japan

Cover: Foto ©Raphael Reischuk / pixelio.de

More available books at **www.hansebooks.com**

Yours always
T. Carlyle

LETTERS

OF

Thomas Carlyle

TO HIS

YOUNGEST SISTER

EDITED WITH AN
INTRODUCTORY
ESSAY BY

CHARLES TOWNSEND COPELAND

LECTURER ON ENGLISH LITERATURE
IN HARVARD UNIVERSITY

WITH PORTRAITS AND OTHER
ILLUSTRATIONS

LONDON
CHAPMAN AND HALL
LIMITED
1899

PREFACE

THE letters printed in this volume were mainly written by Thomas Carlyle to his youngest sister, Mrs. Robert Hanning, who died in Toronto on the thirteenth day of December, 1897. Other members of the family are represented in the correspondence; there are a few letters — these perhaps the most interesting — from Carlyle to his mother; a few, also, from the mother to her oldest and to her youngest child. The collection extends from 1832 to 1890, when Mr. John Carlyle Aitken wrote to inform his aunt, Mrs. Hanning, of the death of James Carlyle, her youngest brother.

The editor of these letters found it desirable to make a careful study of all the published Carlyle documents. The introductory essay on Carlyle as a Letter-Writer grew out of a comparison between Carlyle's correspondence with his family, and his letters to other persons, already printed by Mr. Norton and Mr. Froude.

CONTENTS

LIST OF ILLUSTRATIONS

CARLYLE AS A LETTER-WRITER

MOST persons (perhaps because consciously
or unconsciously they hold the opinion of
George Eliot, that serious subjects should not
be discussed in letters) try to entertain their
correspondents, when they sit down to write
a friendly letter. Famous writers are no exception to this rule. Horace Walpole adapts
his materials with the nicest art; Gray is seldom elegiac in prose; and Chesterfield, not
content with urging his son to " sacrifice
to the Graces," makes his own epistles an
oblation on the altar of those ladies. It is
evident that the younger Pliny chooses his
best stylus, whether a Tuscan villa, or the
eruption of Vesuvius, or a Corinthian statuette form his theme ; and the fact that all is
composed in fear of Cicero and to the glory
of the Latin language cannot have made the
composition less acceptable to his contempo-
raries. The letters of Charles Lamb, the
" argument " of whose life was suited to a
Greek tragedy, must often have carried sun-

shine — quaintly filtered through Lamb's personality — to people who, had they but known it, were far better off than their correspondent. Cowper, the best of English letter-writers, was also one of the most cheerful, and in some of the last communications with his friends, before the darkness had quite settled over him, showed himself touchingly conscious of the social bond. It was nearly always dark with Cowper when he was addressing the Reverend John Newton, the evil genius who tried to be his good genius; but let it be remembered that Cowper wrote to Newton the escape of the hares, — a miniature Gilpin in prose. Most of what came from Olney and Weston, indeed, gave and repeated an impression of sprightly serenity that — except in the letters to Newton — seldom allowed itself to be clouded with the fear which so often kept Cowper trembling. When Madame de Sévigné smiles through her tears, her face turned always toward her daughter, we love her most. We do not feel that she is not making the best of things, but merely that the gayety of her century, thus dashed, is brought nearer the key of our own.

Looked at from this point of view of good spirits, whether real or benevolently feigned,

Carlyle is in blackest contrast to the genial
tradition of letter-writing. As early as when
he was with the Bullers at Kinnaird, he had
frightened his family with an eloquent diag-
nosis of the torments of dyspepsia, and afterward often practiced a becoming caution in
complaining too loudly of anything to them.
Toward the world in general, however, and
toward his brother John — who alone of the
family lived in the world — he seldom observed such care. What he felt, he thought;
and what he thought, he wrote. The denun-
ciatory mood was frequent with Carlyle, and
it would be easy to collect enough of his
secular anathemas for a droll sort of com-
mination service. Men, women, and children,
if they disturbed him, came in for his curse.
All annoyances spoke to Carlyle and his wife
through a megaphone, and were proclaimed
by them through a still larger variety of the
same instrument. Every cock that crowed
near their house was a clarion out of tune,
and the "demon-fowls" were equaled by
dogs, of which each had to their ears the
barking power of Cerberus. When Carlyle
traveled, fierce imprecations upon everything
viatic were wafted back from every stage to
the poor "Goody" in Cheyne Row, often

while she was facing alone the problem of
fresh paint and paper. On the only occasion
I can now recall of Carlyle himself being at
home during repairs, they were to him what
a convulsion of nature would be to most of
us, and his outcries were of cosmic vehemence
and shrillness. In these wild splutterings of
genius, a maid servant was a "puddle," a
"scandalous randy," or even a "sluttish har-
lot;" a man servant was a "flunkey;" and,
if he waked Carlyle too early in the morning,
he was a "flunkey of the devil." Rank,
wealth, and worldly respectability were, it
need not at this day be said, no defense
against these grotesque indictments. The
clergy and lovers of the clergy — unless,
indeed, they happened to be anæmic and
"Socinian" — were always accused of "shov-
el-hattedness." Persons who, from Plato to
Scott, waged no visible warfare with their
own souls, and lived their lives without stated
conversion from "the everlasting No," were
rarely acceptable to Carlyle. Any man of
his acquaintance who, besides being thus at
ease in Zion, had also gathered worldly gear,
was apt, according to Carlyle, to have lost his
humanity in "gigmanity." London, in the
word he gladly borrowed from Cobbett, was

a "monstrous wen;" Europe, "a huge suppuration;" mankind, "mostly fools;" and the world at large, "a dusty, fuliginous chaos."

If, in moods which give forth such words, Carlyle seems to write with a quill plucked from the fretful porpentine, a new book of Lamentations might be gathered from his other frequent and familiar condition. This was the state of body and soul which moved him to sorrow and repining over himself, England, and the world. If he had never made his great success in literature, these wailing cries might plausibly be assigned to the disappointed ambitions of a man whose lot was even more embittered by dyspepsia. But in this respect the tone of the apprentice, throughout a wearifully long apprenticeship, was strangely like that of the past master in literature, who for the last twenty years of his life was the most eminent of English writers. There is doubtless a habit of mourning as of rejoicing, and habit counted for much with Carlyle. Yet what I am disposed to contend is that though Aladdin's lamp had lighted him to a success even earlier than Sheridan's or Kipling's, his books and letters would still from time to time have sounded the whole gamut of Jeremiah. It

was in his Scotch blood that thus they should,
— in his Puritan spirit and his Puritanical
digestion. In short, Carlyle's melancholy
was from temperament far more than from
circumstance, — a spiritual habitude to which
he was destined and born.

See the sparks fly upward in March, 1822 :
" Art is long and life is short; and of the
threescore and ten years allotted to the liver,
how small a portion is spent in anything but
vanity and vice, if not in wretchedness, and
worse than unprofitable struggling with the
adamantine laws of fate ! I am wae when I
think of all this, but it cannot be helped."
More than forty years after, the sad-eyed
victor in his chosen field reminds us that he,
more than most men, is born to trouble. In
1863 he writes to Emerson from Annandale :
"I live in total solitude, sauntering moodily
in thin checkered woods, galloping about,
once daily, by old lanes and roads, oftenest
latterly on the wide expanses of Solway shore
(when the tide is *out!*) where I see bright
busy Cottages far off, houses over even in
Cumberland, and the beautifulest amphithe-
atre of eternal Hills, — but meet no living
creature; and have endless thoughts as loving and as sad and sombre as I like." This

is none the less (perhaps, rather, the more)
sad, for all the wide and shining landscape.
A few lines later Carlyle says: "You perceive
me sufficiently at this point of my Pilgrimage,
as withdrawn to *Hades* for the time being;
intending a month's walk there, till the
muddy semi-solutions settle into sediment
according to what laws they have, and there
be perhaps a partial restoration of clearness."
The voice of 1865, though early in the interim it gained its individual accent, is still
the voice of 1822.

Malice was operant in this choice of a passage from one of Carlyle's letters to Emerson,
to show the frequent hue of his spirit. For
not only is the mere thought of Emerson a
cause of cheer to most men,—to Carlyle himself it usually brought comfort,—but Carlyle
had adopted Emerson, or more nearly adopted
him than any one else except Sterling, into
the close communion of his own family, toward whom he generally showed compunction
in the matter of invective and lament. Yet
in writing to Emerson and to them he would
sometimes forget his restraint, and, while eat-
ing his heart, would invite them to the same
repast. It has been said that Froude made
an exceptionally gloomy selection from Car-

lyle's correspondence, and that Mr. Norton's
volumes give a fairer view of the habitual
tone of his spirits. So far as they are concerned with Emerson and with Carlyle's kindred, an explanation of the higher average of
cheerfulness has already been offered. But
even in these letters, and still more in the
rest of Mr. Norton's selections, one is tempted
to inquire whether he did not intend (and
very properly) to redress the balance which
Froude had unduly weighted on the other
side. For the essence and gist of Carlyle's
published writings — books, letters, and jour-
nals — is that "it is not a merry place, this
world; it is a stern and awful place." Much
that is meat to other men was poison, or tinc-
tured with poison, to him. "My letter, you
will see" (he wrote to his brother John in
1828), "ends in sable, like the life of man.
My own thoughts grow graver every day I
live." He could, and did, suck melancholy
from his own successful lectures, from his
own books and the books of others, from the
state of the nation and the state of his own
health, from society, from solitude. Craigenputtock, high on the moors between Dum-
friesshire and Galloway, and sixteen miles
from the town of Dumfries, has always seemed

to me the right scenic background for Carlyle. The stone farmhouse, surrounded by a
few acres of land reclaimed from peat bog,
stands in the midst of bleak hills, seven hundred feet above the level of the sea. This is
the right scenery for Carlyle, and many of
his most characteristic letters, from whatever
places written, carry with them a feeling of
the north, November, and the moors. Had
Froude left any gaps in his biography, they
might be bridged with sighs.

Persons who talked with Carlyle, or who
heard him talk, often received a different impression. This was, no doubt, partly because
his pentecostal gift excited him to a variety
and fire of speech for which he afterward
paid the penalty of a natural enough reac-
tion ; partly, also, because the sense of humor
never deserted him at those moments, and
rich gusts of laughter swept away boding
prophecy, fierce invective, and the whole symbolic apparatus of Carlylean denunciation.
Humor, indeed, is always to be reckoned with
in Carlyle; and his letters, like his books,
abound in a range of it — seldom genial —
that extends from the grim to the farcical.
But you cannot hear a man laugh in print;
and where in a Carlyle conversation the stage

direction would be, "Exit laughing," in a
Carlyle letter it appears, "Exit groaning" or
"Exit swearing." The writer "laughs off,"
as Macbeth and Macduff "fight off;" and
the reader hears but the ghost of a laugh, —
a faint, imagined reverberation.

Hence, loathèd Melancholy, and a truce to
sable. I have, perhaps, made too much of a
striking characteristic, however indubitable,
of a great writer. The famous rat was not
always gnawing at the pit of his stomach;
and when neither the mood of vituperation
nor the mood of lament was upon him, he
was of too vigorous and too honest a mind
not to discuss with comparative calmness
many subjects that interested him. What
did interest him and what did n't, what appears in his letters and what is never seen
there, would make a catalogue fairly descrip-
tive of Carlyle's intellectual and moral constitution. Food and raiment he seldom writes
of, save as necessities of life. No Christmas
gastronomy in his letters, no rule for "cook-
ing a chub," no incipient essay on roast pig.
As Carlyle's pen is never occupied with cards,
one concludes that "old women to play whist
with of an evening," so much desired by a
certain delightful letter-writer, were not a de-

sideratum with him. Women, in fact, play no dominantly feminine part in his life. Love, as a passion, he apparently does not understand. He gave no more sensitive response to the fine arts than Emerson, in whose books there are many "blind places," — so says Mr. Chapman in his original and important essay on Emerson, — " like the notes which will not strike on a sick piano." To name the theatre is, with Carlyle, to scorn it. Goethe himself could not make him care for plays or play-acting. Goethe's Wilhelm Meister he learned to admire, although, had any other written it, the book would have had from him the treatment it got from Wordsworth. If we may believe Froude, Carlyle called some of the most noteworthy French novels " a new Phallus worship, with Sue, Balzac, and Co. for prophets, and Madame Sand for a virgin." Poetry, art allied to his own, interests Carlyle only through its thought or its lesson. In the actual affairs of life, he desires neither money, rank, nor political power. He gives no adherence to any religious creed, political faith, or party leader. He often feels himself in a " minority of one," but on a certain occasion doubles the number, to include Emerson.

Here may end, without special reason for ending, the catalogue of negatives by which people learn to know Carlyle in his letters. Shorter, not less impressive or informing, is the list of positives. Words Carlyle must have had at least a sneaking fondness for. He does not admit it, but he uses words and phrases in a way that tells its own story to those upon whose ears his noblest strains fall like music. Very often, as he intended, the words stand for facts, which he loved, and for which he was proud to tell his love. Purity, honor, and truth are dear to Carlyle, and he celebrates them in his letters. "Poor and sad humanity," although it often moves him to scorn, never quite loses its hold upon him : his letters are a crowded thoroughfare of human beings, who live again at his touch. Good sayings — pious, shrewd, sage, or humorous, as the case may be — this eloquent talker rolls under his tongue, especially when they are in the speech of the Scottish people. His taste for humor is catholic enough to relish jokes; and he himself, unclannish chiefly in that, jokes without difficulty. Strength of any kind bulks so large in Carlyle's esteem that the historian of Cromwell and Friedrich has often been accused of mak-

ing might his right. After years of what he
felt to be misrepresentation, he endeavored to
set things straight by declaring that right, in
the long run, was pretty sure to be mighty.
However this may be, the strength of contemporary leaders was likely, by his thinking, to
be founded on unrighteousness; and it was
easier for him to worship his heroes through
the long nave of the past. There was an
altar for Cromwell, but — alas that it should
have been so — there was none for Lincoln.

Although these positives are lengthening
themselves out, there must be mention here
of the mother, wife, family, and friends, who
figure so engrossingly in Carlyle's correspondence. I think we gather from the grand
total of documents in the case that he loved
his mother more deeply and singly than he
loved any other person. Yet for his wife
he had a strong, often disquieted affection.
The expression of this in his letters to her,
which are as remarkable for emotion as for
a very high order of writing, is of course
less checkered than it could have been in
the faring together of two such yoke-fel-
lows. In the action of temperament upon temperament, like does not cure like. During
the long episode of Gloriana, it is often pos-

sible to read between the lines of Carlyle's letters to his wife. After the death of the first Lady Ashburton, however, occurs the most striking passage of self-accusation to be found in any letter before the death of Mrs. Carlyle. Carlyle writes to her on the 11th of July, 1858 : —

" All yesterday I remarked, in speaking to ——, if any tragic topic came in sight, I had a difficulty to keep from breaking down in my speech, and becoming inarticulate with emotion over it. It is as if the scales were falling from my eyes, and I were beginning to see in this, my solitude, things that touch me to the very quick. Oh, my little woman ! what a suffering thou hast had, and how nobly borne ! with a simplicity, a silence, courage, and patient heroism which are only now too evident to me. Three waer days I can hardly remember in my life ; but they were not without worth either ; very blessed some of the feelings, though many so sore and miserable. It is very good to be left alone with the truth sometimes, to hear with all its sternness what it will say to one."

It is often to be noted that no great moment finds Carlyle without a great word. Moving as is the utterance just quoted, it is dumb in comparison with this, written after the death of Mrs. Carlyle : " Not for above two days could I estimate the immeasurable depths of it, or the infinite sorrow which had peeled my life all bare, and in a moment shattered my poor world to universal ruin."

Mother, wife, family, and one or two friends, then, were very dear to Carlyle. " Love me a little," he writes once to Emerson. Next to these few persons, nature had perhaps the strongest sway over him; and the strange, beautiful landscapes that shine out from some of his darkest letters would be enough to found a reputation on. The phrases live in one's memory as if they had line and color.

Two main facts detach themselves, I think, from these imperfect suggestions of what Carlyle's letters contain and what they are vacant of. In the first place, no one can doubt that although — except in writing to the Annandale kin — Carlyle seldom attempts to control himself, is seldom interesting or entertaining of set purpose, he is yet, for interest and entertainment, a letter-writer among a thousand. Single-minded and single-hearted, true as the very truth, in the words of his mouth he utters the meditations of his heart. Gifted with eloquence, with humor, with pathos, with eyes that see everything and a memory that loses nothing, with an energy of speech which (compared with that given to the majority of his fellow creatures) is clearly superhuman, Carlyle uses his amazing literary vehicle as an Arabian magic carpet to transport him to his correspondent. The letter is the writer; the word is the man.

So much for one fact. The other, not now stated for the first time, is that Carlyle, in his familiar letters as in his published works, presents the curious combination of mystic and realist. The world that can be tested by the senses is, in Carlyle's belief, only the vesture, sometimes muddy, sometimes clear, of the divine principle. For many readers, the expression of this ruling idea of Carlyle and his work is confused not only by apparently contradictory phrasings, but by the shifting of his conception of God between theism and pantheism. When, however, Carlyle utters himself most earnestly and most characteristically on this cardinal point of his belief, no manner of man can misunderstand him. "Matter," exclaims he, "exists only spiritually, and to represent some idea and

body it forth. Heaven and Earth are but
the time-vesture of the Eternal. The Uni-
verse is but one vast symbol of God; nay, if
thou wilt have it, what is man himself but a
symbol of God? Is not all that he does sym-
bolical, a revelation to sense of the mystic
God-given force that is in him? — a gospel
of Freedom, which he, the 'Messias of Nature,' preaches as he can by act and word."
It was only to be expected that the favorite
quotation of a man whose high belief can be
stated thus, of a man who regarded time as
an illusion, should be the lines from Shakespeare's Tempest : —

> " We are such stuff
> As dreams are made on, and our little life
> Is rounded with a sleep."

Now, although it is proverbially difficult to
prove a negative, the ease with which a negative can be stated should be equally matter
of proverb. Accordingly, we find that Carlyle, in his letters, a hundred times denounces
the world as he sees it for once that he describes, or even suggests, the world as he
would see it. Silent heroes should be the
rulers of England. Silent heroes are rare
birds, even among the dead. Instead of
them, talking parliamentarians are at the

head of things; and Carlyle has to say what he thinks of Gladstone and Disraeli, the alternately ruling talkers. When, in 1874, Disraeli proposed to grant him a pension and bestow on him also the Grand Cross of the Bath, he wrote to John Carlyle: " I do, however, truly admire the magnanimity of Dizzy in regard to me. He is the only man I almost never spoke of except with contempt."

Men of letters fare no better than men of action. They should be priests, in white, unspotted robes. What does Carlyle find them? In 1824, after pinning Coleridge, De Quincey, Hazlitt, and Leigh Hunt fiercely to the page, he writes to Miss Welsh: " ' Good heavens!' I often inwardly exclaim, ' and is this the literary world?' This rascal rout, this dirty rabble, destitute not only of high feeling and knowledge or intellect, but even of common honesty! The very best of them are ill-natured weaklings. They are not red-blooded men at all. . . . Such is the literary world of London; indisputably the poorest part of its population at present." So Carlyle wrote of writers when he was putting on his literary armor, and not very differently when he was putting it off. His Hero as Man of Letters was almost invariably seen at

a distance, either of time or space. He
spitted Coleridge on his sharpest spear, and
two blasting, withering descriptions of Charles
Lamb — with forty years between them for
reflection — remain to the everlasting hurt
of Carlyle's own reputation.

Vitriol blesseth neither him that gives nor
him that takes, yet Carlyle stayed to the end
of his many days essentially high-minded.
Honorable, simple, helpful, charitable in deed
though not in word, he was seen at the limit
of his course to have a better heart, a character less deteriorated, than many a man — no
less good at the start — who has indulged
himself with " omitting the negative proposi-
tion."   The habit of scorn would in the long
run have been more harmful to character than
the habit of tolerance and facile praise, except that Carlyle had an extraordinarily high
standard of principle and performance, and
held to it not only in his judgment of others,
but also in what he exacted of himself.   The
fact that Carlyle never tried to reconcile the
inconsistency (as it may have seemed to some
persons) between the Deity of his worship and
the symbolic manifestations of that Deity in a
world so little to Carlyle's liking no doubt
helped him to keep his spiritual integrity.

In company and contrast with the mysticism of Carlyle's thought — "idealism" is the better word, if it be strictly interpreted — is the eager realism of his literary methods. As a result of this piquant union, Carlyle means one thing to one man, and another, quite different thing to another man. The Carlyle of X, the strait idealist, is a moonish philosopher, to be shunned by A, the strait realist, who rejoices in the closely packed narrative, the wild action, and the portraits of men and women, that make but a trivial appeal to X. This union of natures is plain enough in Shakespeare, in whom nothing surprises. The hand which gave us the Tempest gave us also Juliet's nurse and Hotspur's description of "a certain Lord." Too often, however, the idealist's grasp of the concrete is wavering and intermittent; too often the soul of the realist needs little feeding.

Carlyle vibrated between these two elements of his nature, and fortified one with the other. When, after burrowing in the dust-heap of the past or fishing into "the general Mother of Dead Dogs," he had brought to light some pearl (or, it might be, only some oyster-shell) of fact, he often improved the opportunity to show the larger significance of the little gleam or glint of reality. It was the defect of a fine quality that, in his later work, and especially in Frederick, he spent himself on irrelevant facts which helped to make Carlyle's longest book a splendid failure, with episodes of indubitable success.

The looser form of the letter more properly admits the isolated concrete. Shrewd, welcome bits of fact are everywhere in Carlyle's letters; everywhere, too, are those other expressions of a great realist, — vividly " composed " elements of landscape, and portraits that give every token of life except breath. As with every artist, whatever he depicts takes color from him, and is seen through his temperament. In the summer of 1837 Carlyle writes to Sterling from Scotsbrig : " One night, late, I rode through the village where I was born. The old kirkyard tree, a huge old gnarled ash, was nestling itself softly against the great twilight in the north. A star or two looked out, and the old graves were all there, and my father and my sister; and God was above us all." Here be worn, familiar things. Gray has been to the village churchyard at the hour of parting day, and a procession has followed in his footsteps. But this kirkyard, where Carlyle has since laid himself down with his kindred, is Carlyle's.

The reappearance (usually heightened or elaborated) of bits of prospect or topography first recorded in Carlyle's letters is an interesting characteristic of his writing. His first visit to Paris was of much service to him in fixing the places and scenes of The French Revolution; the trip into the country of Cromwell's birth and the examination of Naseby field come into sight again in the book, — witness especially the "Cease your fooling," and the troopers' teeth that bit into Carlyle's memory; and a number of rough drafts for details of Frederick appear in letters from the Continent. A brief note, during a visit to Mr. Redwood in 1843, of the Glamorganshire "green network of intricate lanes, mouldering ruins, vigorous vegetation good and bad," was afterward dilated (in the Life of Sterling) into the spacious and beautiful landscape beginning: "Llanblethian hangs pleasantly, with its white cottages, and orchard and other trees, on the western slope of a green hill; looking far and wide over green meadows and little or bigger hills, in the pleasant plain of Glamorgan."

Distinguished as are Carlyle's portraits of

places, it is probably his portraits of persons
that abide longest and most completely in
the memories of most readers. Robespierre,
Mirabeau and Mirabeau *père*, Frederick and
Frederick William, — it is one sign of Carlyle's power that he can make subordinate
characters salient and still bring out his hero,
— Voltaire, Cromwell, and the Abbot Sam-
son, are a few of the pictures that line his
galleries. Wonderful as are these render-
ings of men he never saw, his sketches of men
he had known are almost literally "speaking
likenesses." Coleridge, Leigh Hunt, Dickens,
Thackeray, Tennyson, Mazzini, Louis Napoleon, are among the many who are painted to
a miracle in Carlyle's letters. Behold a great
American, in a letter to Emerson : —

"Not many days ago I saw at breakfast
the notablest of all your Notabilities, Daniel
Webster. He is a magnificent specimen;
you might say to all the world, This is your
Yankee Englishman, such Limbs we make in
Yankee-land! As a Logic-fencer, Advocate,
or Parliamentary Hercules, one would incline
to back him at first sight against all the
extant world. The tanned complexion, that
amorphous craglike face; the dull black eyes
under their precipice of brows, like dull an-

thracite furnaces, needing only to be blown;
the mastiff-mouth, accurately closed : — I
have not traced as much of silent Berserker-
rage, that I remember of, in any other man.
'I guess I should not like to be your nigger!'"

At the risk of numbering this paper with
the books of Chrysippus, we must look again
at the portrait of De Quincey, which is, perhaps, the artist's chief triumph. Although
it is to be found in the Reminiscences, it yet
belongs here well enough, for that book is
not so much a book as a long, rambling letter, partly of remorse, partly of pity, from
Carlyle to himself. "He was a pretty little
creature," says this terrible, sad old man, re-
membering after forty years, "full of wire-
drawn ingenuities; bankrupt enthusiasms,
bankrupt pride; with the finest silver-toned
low voice, and most elaborate gently-winding
courtesies and ingenuities of conversation :
'What would n't one give to have him in a
Box, and take him out to talk !' (That was
Her criticism of him; and it was right good.)
A bright, ready and melodious talker; but
in the end an inconclusive and long-winded.
One of the smallest man-figures I ever saw;
shaped like a pair of tongs; and hardly above
five feet in all : when he sat, you would have

taken him, by candle-light, for the beautifullest little Child ; blue-eyed, blonde-haired,
sparkling face, — had there not been a something too, which said, ' Eccovi, this Child has
been in Hell!' " One would be sure, without
other evidence than " *Her* criticism " in this
description, which is also a " character," — to
use the old word, — that *She*, too, had been
terrible. The broken order, the curious punc-
tuation, the capitals and italics, the leave of
absence granted to the verb, the quick inter-
jections, all taken together make the passage
a concentrated example of Carlyle's *vox hu-
mana* style, — of his writing when it is most
like speech, sublimated.

In his use of persons, as of places, there
are pregnant comparisons to be made between
Carlyle's first study and the final portrait.
Sterling and old Sterling are cases in point;
Coleridge, maybe, the best instance of all.
The main lines and the personal atmosphere,
always visible, I think, in the sketch, are
reproduced by Carlyle in the finished work.
But in the heightening of lights, in the deep-
ening of shade, in composition, above all, he
makes many changes, which almost invariably
result in greater intensity of effect.

From such comparisons, if patiently con-

ducted, might come luminous comment on
the question of Carlyle's style, — a question
more vexed than the Bermoothes.

So far and so much for Carlyle's general
aspect as a letter-writer. I have tried to show
that, in addressing himself to a very few
friends, and especially to his own family, he
displays a different set of qualities. The difference between his vehemence toward the
world at large and his gentleness toward his
mother sometimes seems as marked as that
between the two visions of the prophet Jeremiah : the one a seething caldron, the face
thereof from the north; the other, a rod of
an almond tree. The world, in truth, for this
peasant of genius, was, to the considerable
degree in which he remained a peasant, an
assemblage of persons and things to be ap-
proached with many reserves and a deal of
more or less violent disapproval. Annandale,
contrariwise, was an honest, strength-giving
corner of the world, which did for him
through life the office of the earth to An-
tæus. He went back to it so often that he
never lost his native accent, and, in certain
respects, the point of view to which he was
born. So long as Carlyle's mother lived,
there was rarely a year in which he did not

make a pilgrimage to Scotsbrig; and, after she died, he went oftener to her grave than most sons, dwelling at a distance from their mothers, visit them in life. Scotsbrig also came to him in the shape of letters, as well as in the unsentimental (though, rightly beheld, not unpathetic) guise of oatmeal, bacon, clothes, and what not. The Carlyles held that good meal could not be bought in London; and when the barrel wasted, it was filled again from home. One far-brought fowl we all remember as the epic subject of a letter from Mrs. Carlyle in Chelsea to her sister-in-law in Scotland. Carlyle had his clothes made in Annan, partly from thrift, partly from distrust of London tailors.

However much he depended on the people and the kindly fruits of his native soil, however much the exclusiveness of the Carlyles may have been only that common to all Scotch peasant families, it is still hard to credit, though on the excellent authority of Mrs. Oliphant, that their mutual love was not " by ordinar," even among Scotch peasants. Especially is it difficult of credence that the attachment of Carlyle and his mother was not as rare as it was beautiful. In 1832, after the death of his father, he writes to his

brother Alick, at Scotsbrig : " O let us all be
gentle, obedient, loving to our Mother, now
that she is left wholly to our charge! ' Honour thy Father and thy Mother ' : doubly
honour thy Mother when she alone remains."
For twenty years this double honor was more
than trebly paid. The son writes once to his
mother : " Since I wrote last I have been in
Scotsbrig more than in London." And so
it often is to the end, — and after. Dream-
ing and waking, he looks far up across England and the Solway. In the spring the plow
and the sower pass between his eyes and the
page of Cromwell or The French Revolution;
in the autumn he has a vision of the yellow fields, of " Jamie's " peat-stack, and the
" cauldron " singing under his mother's window. The mother's trembling thought of her
children answers their love for her. " She
told me the other day " (writes one of Carlyle's sisters), " the first gaet she gaed every
morning was to London, then to Italy, then
to Craigenputtock, and then to Mary's, and
finally began to think them at hame were,
maybe, no safer than the rest. When I asked
her what she wished me to say to you, she
said she had a thousand things to say if she
had you here ; ' and thou may tell them, I 'm
very little fra' them.' "

As from his first clear earnings Carlyle sent his father a pair of spectacles, and his mother "a little sovereign to keep the fiend out of her hussif," so throughout he never forgot her in the least or the greatest particular. From year to year he sent her money and tobacco, — which they often smoked together in the farmhouse, — books and comforts and letters. The letters, of course, were far the best of all to her. Often as they came, they could not come often enough. In 1824 Margaret Carlyle wrote to her son: "Pray do not let me want food; as your father says, I look as if I would eat your letters. Write everything and soon." Everything and soon it always was; and in these many letters Carlyle strove to bring near to the untraveled ones at home all that he was seeing and doing. One means of doing this was to describe interesting places in terms of Annandale. Thus, in telling his sister Jean about Naseby, he wrote : —

"Next day they drove me over some fifteen miles off to see the field of Naseby fight — Oliver Cromwell's chief battle, or one of his chief. It was a grand scene for me — Naseby, a venerable hamlet, larger than Middlebie, all built of mud, but trim with high peaked roofs, and two feet thick of smooth thatch on them, and plenty of trees scattered round and among. It is built as on the brow of the Hagheads at Ecclefechan; Cromwell lay with his back to that, and King Charles was drawn up as at Wull Welsh's — only the Sinclair burn must be mostly dried, and the hollow much wider and deeper."

Carlyle knew that his mother would be eager to hear of Luther and Lutherland. In September of the last year but one of her life, he writes to her from Weimar that "Eisenach is about as big as Dumfries;" that a hill near by is "somewhat as Lockerbie hill is in height and position." The donjon tower of the Wartburg (which he translates for her, Watch Castle) stands like the old Tower of Repentance on Hoddam Hill, where his mother had visited him during his "russet-coated idyll" there, many years before. "They open a door, you enter a little apartment, less than your best room at Scotsbrig, I almost think less than your smallest, a very poor low room with an old leaded lattice window; to me the most venerable of all rooms I ever entered." That afternoon they drive to Gotha in a "kind of clatch." Carlyle helps out his English for

his mother with bits of their common Doric,
and falls unconsciously into Scotch locutions,
such as " you would be going," or " you
would be doing," when he means " you are
likely to go " or " likely to do." In larger
matters it is the same. Carlyle may have
been chanting the Miserere to some correspondent, but if he writes to his mother on
the same day, the note changes to Sursum
corda, even though it must visibly struggle
up from the depths. Nor do the Immensities
and the Eternities appear in his letters to her.
In these the Lord her God is also his God.

The belief in personal immortality came to
Carlyle, so far as I can discover, but dimly
and infrequently. This chill lack of faith,
so common in our day, sharpened the dread
of his mother's death. So early as 1844 he
writes in his Journal : " My dear old mother
has, I doubt, been often poorly this winter.
They report her well at present : but, alas !
there is nothing in all the earth so stern to
me as that constantly advancing inevitability,
which indeed has terrified me all my days."
Yet, in Carlyle's letters after her death, a
dovelike peace seems to brood over his deep
sorrow. With Roman piety he records the
death-trance, sixteen hours long, in which his

mother, her face " as that of a statue," lay waiting for the end.   It was another

"Dulcis et alta quies, placidæque simillima morti;"

and all Carlyle's words about that holy parting are grave and sweet.

Whatever of loveliness there may have been in the life together of Carlyle and his wife, — and there was much, in spite of all that has been said to the contrary, — in death they were far divided. She lies with her gentle forbears in the abbey kirk at Haddington; he, in Ecclefechan kirkyard with his peasant forbears. When Carlyle was dying, the Lord remembered for him the kindness of his youth, — his mother might have believed, — and "his mind seemed to turn altogether to the old Ecclefechan days." Said his niece, Mrs. Alexander Carlyle, writing just after his death : "He often took Alick for his father (uncle Sandy), and he would put his arms round my neck and say to me, 'My dear mother.' "

Great writer as Carlyle is, many critics feel that he can never become classical. The word " classic," as Sainte-Beuve has pointed out, is a stretchable term ; but very possibly the Soudanese lexicographer, descended from a native of New Zealand, will label many of Carlyle's phrases " post-classical," and place him with Browning and Ruskin, who felt his influence, in the Silver Age of English. Certainly, the Soudanese Quintilian will do well to tell his pupils the story of Erasmus's ape, and warn them against the danger of imitating Carlyle. Classical or post-classical, Carlyle's name is as closely linked with the French Revolution and the Life of Oliver Cromwell, as is the name of Thucydides with the Peloponnesian War, that of Tacitus with the Emperors of the Julian line, or that of Gibbon with the Decline and Fall of their Empire. Yet even if Carlyle's historical titles were torn from his grant of immortality, he would survive as one of the most remarkable of English letter-writers.

LETTERS OF THOMAS CARLYLE TO HIS YOUNGEST SISTER

LETTERS OF THOMAS CARLYLE TO HIS YOUNGEST SISTER

LETTERS

———

Mrs. Hanning (Janet Carlyle) was born, as were all her brothers and sisters before her, in the village of Ecclefechan. The following notes of her life are supplied by her son-in-law, the Rev. George M. Franklin:—

"She was reckoned the neatest seamstress of the family, and received the rare compliment of praise from her eldest brother (Thomas Carlyle) for having done excellent work on some shirts. Robert Hanning, an old friend of the Carlyles, going to the same school with Janet, and 'looking on the same book,' wooed and won her. They were married at Scotsbrig, on March 15, 1836. They went to Manchester, England, to live, as Mr. Hanning was employed by a Mr. Craig, and subsequently was a partner in the business. This business having proved unprofitable, they returned to Scotland, and Mr. Hanning entered into business with his brother Peter as partner. This proved also a failure. Soon afterward the family went back to Dumfries. Mr. Hanning sailed for America, arriving at New York; and after working there for a time left that city for Hamilton, Ontario, his future home. Mrs. Hanning and her two children remained in Dumfries, although she had wished much to go with her husband and share his fortunes. Thomas persuaded her, ' against her judgment,' as she has said, to wait until her husband was settled. Mr. Hanning was a man of strong convictions and the highest moral principle. The reunion of his family was effected in 1851, when the wife and two daughters left Glasgow in a sailing-vessel, the passage to Quebec occupying about seven weeks. Then taking a steamer from Quebec, they reached Hamilton in good time. This was before the building of the Great Western Railway. Mrs. Hanning soon made a home for her devoted husband, earning the commendation ' brave little sister.' Mr. Hanning entered the service of the Great Western Railway of Canada in 1853, and remained with that company until his death, which occurred March 12, 1878."

An indispensable guide to the correspondence will be found in the following list, given by Professor Norton, of the children of James Carlyle, with the dates of their births, — Thomas, born December 4, 1795 (died at Chelsea, February 5, 1881) ; Alexander, born August 4, 1797 ; Janet, born September 2, 1799 ; John Aitkin, born July 7, 1801 ; Margaret, born September 20, 1803 ; James, born November 12, 1805 ; Mary, born February 2, 1808 ; Jean, born September 2, 1810 ; Janet (Mrs. Hanning), born July 18, 1813.

Among the persons mentioned by Mr. Franklin as visiting Mrs. Hanning, the most distinguished was Emerson, who went to Hamilton in the summer of 1865. " Mr. Emerson placed her in a chair near the window, so that he might the more readily examine her features, and, looking into her eyes, exclaimed, ' And so this is Carlyle's little sister ! ' "

Mention of " the youngest stay of the house, little Jenny," is rare and slight in the published letters and memorials of Carlyle. Froude, in an ingeniously careless passage, confuses her with an older sister, Jean. He speaks of " the youngest child of all, Jane, called the Craw, or Crow, from her black hair." Carlyle, on pages 92 and 93 of the

second volume of the Reminiscences, — in
Mr. Norton's edition, — mentions both Jean
and Jenny: " There was a younger and
youngest sister (Jenny), who is now in Canada ; of far inferior ' speculative intellect ' to
Jean, but who has proved to have (we used
to think) superior housekeeping faculties to
hers."

" My prayers and affection are with you
all, from little Jenny upwards to the head
of the house," writes Carlyle to his mother
on October 19, 1826, after a form common
enough, with its variations, in his early letters. Occasionally she has done something
to be noted. On October 20, 1827 : " Does
Jenny bring home her medals yet ? " On
November 15 : " Does Jenny still keep her
medals ? Tell her that I still love her, and
hope to find her a good lassie and to do her
good." In the spring of 1828 Carlyle writes
from Scotsbrig to his " Dear Little Craw "
in Edinburgh : " Mag and Jenny are here ;
Jenny at the Sewing-school with Jessie Combe,
and making *great* progress." Mrs. Carlyle
adds, in a postscript to an 1835 letter to Mrs.
Aitken : " Carlyle has the impudence to say
he forgot to send his compliments to Jenny ;
as if it were possible for any one acquainted

with that morsel of perfections to *forget* her!
Tell her I will write a letter with my own
hand, and hope to see her 'an ornament to
society in every direction.'"   In a preface —
written many years after — to a letter to Jean
Carlyle, bearing date November, 1825, and
signed Jane Baillie Welsh, Carlyle explains :
" This Jean Carlyle is my second youngest
sister, then a little child of twelve. The
youngest sister, youngest of us all, was Jenny
[Janet], now Mrs. Robert Hanning, in Hamilton, Canada West. These little beings, in
their bits of grey speckled [black and white]
straw bonnets, I recollect as a pair of neat,
brisk items, tripping about among us that
summer at the Hill."   Letter and preface are
given by Froude, as is also a letter from Carlyle to his wife, dated Scotsbrig, May 3, 1842,
and ending thus : " Yesterday I got my hair
cropped, partly by my own endeavours in the
front, chiefly by sister Jenny's in the rear.
I fear you will think it rather an original
cut."

In 1827 : " Tell her that I still love her,
and hope to find her a good lassie and to do
her good ; " in 1873, in Carlyle's last letter
to Mrs. Hanning written with his own hand :
" I please myself with the thought that you

will accept this little New Year's Gift from me as a sign of my unalterable affection, wh[h], tho' it is obliged to be silent (unable to *write* as of old), cannot fade away until I myself do! Of that be always sure, my dear little Sister; and that if in anything I can be of help to you or yours, I right willingly will."

All the letters that follow are strung on a slender thread of biography. Even readers who know their Carlyle thoroughly may like to see, from year to year and from page to page, the contrast between his life in the world and his life with the peasant kindred who were so far from everything that men call the world. And although nothing in these letters will add to our knowledge of Carlyle, they cannot — taken together — fail to touch us freshly with the sense of what he was to his people, and what they were to him.

Carlyle's life until 1832, the year of the first letter, may be most briefly summarized. The son of James Carlyle, a stone-mason, he was born at Ecclefechan, " in a room inconceivably small," on the 4th of December, 1795. He went to school at Annan, and, in 1809, to the University of Edinburgh. Five years later he returned to the Annan school

ECCLEFECHAN, BIRTHPLACE OF THOMAS CARLYLE

as a teacher of mathematics, and in 1816
went to Kirkcaldy to teach the same subject.
After an experience of literary hack work in
Edinburgh, which began when he was twenty-
three years old, he became tutor in the Buller
family. A long, strange, and ill-boding court-
ship ended, on the 17th of October, 1826, in
his marriage with Jane Baillie Welsh. She
had a small inherited estate at Craigenputtock, high up on the moors, and sixteen miles
from Dumfries; and there, two years after
their marriage, they went to live for six years.
In 1831 and 1832 they were merely trying
their wings in London.

"Mrs. Welsh" was Mrs. Carlyle's mother.
"Maister Cairlill" was a frequent name for
Carlyle's brother James. The family had
been living at Scotsbrig since 1826. Carlyle
was thirty-six years old, and his sister nineteen, when the following letter was written.

I. CARLYLE TO JANET CARLYLE, SCOTSBRIG.

Ampton St., London,
23rd January, 1832.

My dear Jenny, — Will you put up with
the smallest of letters rather than with none
at all? I have hardly a moment, and no
paper but this thick, coarse sort.

Understand always, My dear Sister, that I love you well, and am very glad to see and hear that you conduct yourself as you ought. To you also, my little lassie, it is of *infinite* importance how you behave : were you to get a Kingdom, or twenty Kingdoms, it were but a pitiful trifle compared with this, whether you walked as God command you, and did your duty to God and to all men. You have a whole Life before you, to make much of or to make little of: see you choose the *better part*, my dear little sister, and make yourself and all of us pleased with you. I will add no more, but commend you from the heart (as we should all do one another) to God's keeping. May He ever bless you ! I am too late, and must not wait another minute. We have this instant had a long letter from Mrs. Welsh, full of kindness to our Mother and all of you. The Cheese, &c., &c., is faithfully commemorated as a " noble " one ; Mary is also made kind mention of. You did all very right on that occasion. Mrs. Welsh says she must come down to Scotsbrig and see you all. What will you think of that ? Her Father, in the meantime, is very ill, and gives her in-cessant labour and anxiety.

See to encourage Jean to write, and do

you put your hand a little to the work.
What does Maister Cairlill think of the last
letter he wrote us? Was it not a letter
among many? He is a graceless man. I
send you a portrait of one of our Chief Radi-
cals here: it is said to be very like.

I remain always, My dear Sister,
Your affectionate
T. CARLYLE.

On January 24, — Froude gives the date
wrongly as the 26th, — the day after the date
of this letter, Carlyle, still in London, heard
of the death of his father, at the age of sev-
enty-three. He wrote immediately to his mother in terms which place the letter high even
among his letters; and in less than a week he
had uttered the wail of genius that stands
first in the Reminiscences, — a book which
has "no language but a cry." By April he
was back again at Craigenputtock, where it
was so still that poor Mrs. Carlyle could hear
the sheep nibbling a quarter of a mile away.
Carlyle had now a new grief in the death of
Goethe, who, making of him a disciple, had
left him a teacher on his own account. The
loss of Goethe found a measurable compensa-
tion in correspondence with Mill, who had

been kindled into something very like fire by
Carlyle's review of Croker's Boswell, just
published in Fraser's Magazine. It is one of
the greatest of Carlyle's briefer performances,
although written at short notice. " Carlyle,"
said his wife, " always writes well when he
writes fast." This essay, indeed, has a high
place in the development of an idea which
may be stated as Croker's Boswell, Macaulay's
Boswell, Carlyle's Boswell, and — Boswell.

There followed now essays on Goethe and
Ebenezer Elliott's Corn Law Rhymes (Carlyle's last contribution to the Edinburgh
Review), and a highly important article on
Diderot for the Foreign Quarterly. In the
autumn of 1832, Carlyle notes that the
money from the essay on Goethe has gone
in part payment of Jeffrey's loan, that Craigenputtock has grown too lonely even for him,
and that his literary plans demand a library.
Not only must the work on Diderot have
assured him of his ability to fuse and weld
the most stubborn materials, but it opened
his eyes to the French Revolution as a subject for his pen. Moved, then, by weariness
of the solitude *à deux* among the peat moss,
and by this new purpose in writing, the twain
removed to Edinburgh toward the end of
1832.

Four months of Edinburgh were enough
to convince Carlyle that here was for him no
continuing city; enough, also, to enable him
to collect and carry back to Craigenputtock
the substance of The Diamond Necklace, one
of the best of his tragi-comic pieces.

The loneliness of "the whinstone strong-
hold" on the moors was cheered in the following August by Emerson's memorable visit.
"We went out to walk over long hills,"
writes Emerson in English Traits, "and
looked at Criffel, then without his cap, and
down into Wordsworth's country. There we
sat down and talked of the immortality of
the soul."

The essay on Cagliostro, written in March,
1833, was printed in Fraser's Magazine for
July and August; and Fraser agreed to publish Sartor Resartus in the next volume,
"only fining Carlyle eight guineas a sheet
for his originality." This gadfly tax on genius; the Foreign Quarterly's refusal of The
Diamond Necklace, patently a masterpiece
though it was; Jeffrey's refusal to recommend Carlyle for a professorship of astron-
omy; and, by way of climax, the defection of
one of those maids whose misdemeanors continue a servile war through so many of the

Carlyle chronicles, directed Carlyle's gaze
toward what Johnson thought the fairest
prospect ever spread before a Scotchman.
Emerson had observed that " he was already
turning his eyes towards London with a
scholar's appreciation," and at last, on the
25th of February, 1834, Carlyle wrote to his
brother John : " We learned incidentally last
week that Grace, our servant, though ' without fault to us,' and whom we, with all her
inertness, were nothing but purposing to
keep, had resolved on 'going home next summer.' The cup that had long been filling ran
over with the smallest of drops. After meditating on it for a few minutes, we said to one
another : 'Why not *bolt* out of all these sooty
despicabilities, of *Kerrays* and lying draggle-
tails of byre-women, and peat-moss and iso-
lation and exasperation and confusion, and
go at once to London ? ' *Gedacht, gethan !*
Two days after we had a letter on the road
to Mrs. Austin, to look out among the
' houses to let' for us, and an advertisement
to Mac Diarmid to try for the letting of our
own." Cattle, poultry, and various superflui-
ties, were sold. Carlyle went on ahead, and
was guided by the airy steps of Leigh Hunt,
then a dweller in Upper Cheyne Row, Chel-

sea, to the house Number 5, Great Cheyne
Row, which the new tenants soon made interesting to much of what was best in London
(to much, also, Mrs. Oliphant has taken pains
to say, of what was not the best), and event-
ually to the English-speaking world. The
house was not taken until Mrs. Carlyle had
inspected and approved it. A few days after
the 10th of June, the date of their installa-
tion, Carlyle wrote to his mother: " We lie
safe at a bend of the river, away from all the
great roads; have air and quiet hardly inferior to Craigenputtock, an outlook from the
back windows into mere leafy regions, with
here and there a red high-peaked old roof
looking through; and see nothing of London,
except by day the summits of St. Paul's Cathedral and Westminster Abbey, and by night
the gleam of the great Babylon affronting
the peaceful skies. The house itself is probably the best we have ever lived in, a right
old, strong, roomy brick-house, built near
one hundred and fifty years ago, and likely
to see three races of these modern fashiona-
bles fall before it comes down." It all sounds
like a sunny backwater, but in truth the Carlyles had taken a very bold plunge into the
world-sea. Their reserve of money could have

been, at the utmost, no more than three hundred pounds ; and the only personal sign of
the times for them was the fact that the
writer of Sartor — now coming out in chapters — was thought a literary maniac, and
that Fraser feared the ruin of his magazine.

The household gods, however, once tem-
pled in Cheyne Row, were never carried back
across the Border ; nor, in fact, were they,
in the half-century of life that remained to
Carlyle, removed to any other spot. Here he
caught the last glimpse of Edward Irving,
the friend of his youth ; here he welcomed
Sterling, " a new young figure," the closest
friend of his middle life ; and hither came to
him Froude and Ruskin, his latest followers.

At first, in the chosen habitation, it was
" desperate hope " and " bitter thrift." The
readers of Fraser's Magazine received Sartor
each month with renewed disgust. " Sartor,"
said the publisher, " excites universal disap-
probation." While this passionate history of
a soul, with its motive so strangely drawn
from the Holy Bible and the great, unholy
Dean, was waiting to touch the slow spirit of
the British reading public, Carlyle — taking
counsel of his necessities, his ambition, and
his inspirations — applied himself to the his-

tory of the French Revolution. The first volume — as all the world knows — was lent in manuscript to Mill, who lent it to Mrs. Taylor, his "veevid" and "iridescent" Egeria, whose servant kindled fires with it. Carlyle had not been offered, as he thought he should have been, the editorship of the new London and Westminster Review; and Mill, for fear of his father, did not dare even to give him work to do for it. Carlyle himself had refused to sell his independence to the Times. There was thus nothing for it but to rewrite the burnt volume, of which he had kept no notes. With such vigor did he drive his mind and his pen that the lost chapters were restored by September 22, 1835. Mill had told him of the loss on the 6th of the preceding March. Mrs. Carlyle wrote to her sister-in-law, Mrs. Aitken, in August: " I do not think that the second version is, on the whole, inferior to the first; it is a little less vivacious, perhaps, but better thought and put together. One chapter more brings him to the end of his second ' first volume,' and then we shall sing a Te Deum and get drunk; for which, by the way, we have unusual facilities at present, a friend (Mr. Wilson) having yesterday sent us a present of a hamper (some six or seven pounds' worth) of the finest old Madeira wine."

Better yet than wine was an American edition of Sartor, godfathered by Emerson, to the number of five hundred copies. This was in April, 1836, and another edition was soon demanded. Carlyle amused himself by quoting the book, in his essay on Mirabeau, as the work of a New England writer.

"The Doctor," mentioned in the letter to follow, was Carlyle's brother John, who, thanks to Jeffrey, had been for some years traveling physician to Lady Clare. "Anne Cook" was an Annandale servant whom Carlyle brought with him on his return from Scotsbrig, in October, 1835. Mrs. Carlyle wrote of Anne Cook, "She amuses me every hour of the day with her perfect incomprehension of everything like ceremony;" and several of her homespun sayings became proverbs in Cheyne Row. "Short," as Carlyle uses it in writing to his sister, has apparently the meaning often attached to it in New England, — "short of temper." The whole sentence bears a quizzing reference to the year before, when, on the 4th of June, Carlyle had written: "Alick, writing to me yesterday, mentions among other things that you

are *shorted* (as he phrases it) because I have
not written. . . . Do not you *shorten*, my
dear little Bairn, but *lengthen*, and know that
if you take anything amiss, it is for mere
want of seeing how it really was; that of all
delusions Satan could tempt you with, that
of wanting my brotherly affection, now and
always while we inhabit the Earth together,
is the most delusive." And on the 23d of
December: "Do not shorten, but lengthen."

The "second volume" is, of course, the
second volume of The French Revolution.
Of both first and second Carlyle had written
more vehemently to Emerson, a few weeks
before: "I got the fatal First Volume finished (in the miserablest way, after great
efforts) in October last; my head was all in
a whirl; I fled to Scotland and my Mother
for a month of rest. Rest is nowhere for the
Son of Adam; all looked so 'spectral' to me
in my old-familiar Birthland; Hades itself
could not have seemed stranger; Annandale
also was part of the kingdom of Time. Since
November I have worked again as I could;
a second volume got wrapped up and sealed
out of my sight within the last three days.
There is but a Third now: one pull more,
and then! It seems to me, I will fly into

some obscurest cranny of the world, and lie silent there for a twelvemonth. The mind is weary, the body is very sick; a little black speck dances to and fro in the left eye (part of the retina protesting against the liver, and striking work). I cannot help it; it must flutter and dance there, like a signal of distress, unanswered till I be done. My familiar friends tell me farther that the Book is all wrong, style, cramp, &c., &c. My friends, I answer, you are very right; but this also, Heaven be my witness, I cannot help. — In such sort do I live here; all this I had to write you, if I wrote at all."

The contrast between such a passage and the whole letter to his sister is but one of a multitude of instances that show the change in Carlyle's spirit whenever he sat down to write to his home people.

II. CARLYLE TO MRS. HANNING. MANCHESTER.

5 Cheyne Row, Chelsea, London,
16th May, 1836.

My dear Jenny, — Your letter has been here several weeks, a very welcome messenger to us, and I did not think at the time I should have been so long in answering it. But I have been drawn hither and thither by

many things, of late; besides, I judged that
Robert and you were happy enough of your-
selves for the present, and did not much need
any foreign aid or interruption. I need not
assure you, my dear little Jenny, of the interest I took in the great enterprise you had
embarked on ; of my wishes and prayers
that it might prove for the good of both.
On the whole, I can say that, to my judgment, it looks all very fair and well. You
know I have all along regarded Hanning as
an uncommonly brisk, glegg little fellow since
the first time I saw him (hardly longer than
my leg, then), and prophesied handsome
things of him in the world. It is very rare
and very fortunate when two parties that have
affected each other from childhood upwards
get together in indissoluble partnership at
last. May it prove well for you, as I think
it will. You must take the good and the
ill in faithful mutual help, and, whoever or
whatever fail you, never fail one another. I
have no doubt Robert will shift his way with
all dexterity and prudence thro' that Cotton
Babylon, looking sharp about him ; knowing
always, too, that " honesty is the best policy "
for all manner of men. Do thou faithfully
second him, my bairn : that will be the best
of lots for thee.

I think it possible that now and then, especially when you are left alone, the look of so many foreign things may seem dispiriting to you, and the huge smoke and stour of that tumultuous Manchester (which is not unlike the uglier parts of London) produce quite other than a pleasant impression. But take courage, my woman, " you will use, you will use," and get hefted to the place, as all creatures do. There are many good people in that vast weaving - shop, many good things among the innumerable bad. Keep snug within your own doors, keep your own hearth snug; by and by you will see what is worth venturing out for. Have nothing to do with the foolish, with the vain and ill-conducted. Attach yourself to the well-living and sensible, to every one from whom you find there is real benefit derivable. Thus, by degrees a desirable little circle will form itself around you; you will feel that Manchester is a home, as all places under the heavenly sun here may become for one.

In a newspaper you would notice that the Doctor was come. Till this day, almost. there was little else to be said about him than that he was here and well. He has been speculating and enquiring as to what he should do,

and now has determined that London practice
will not do for the present; that he should
go back with his Lady and try again to get
practice there. He is gone out this moment
to make a bargain to that effect. They are
to set out for Rome again on the first of September; from that till the first of March the
Doctor is Lady Clare's doctor, but lives in his
own lodging at Rome; after that he is free to
do whatsoever he will: to stay there, if they
seem inviting; to return home, if otherwise.
I believe, myself, that he has decided wisely.
Till September, then, we have him amongst
us. He talks of being "off in a week or
two" for Scotland; he charged me to say
that he would see Manchester, and you, either
as he went or as he returned. It is not much
out of the way, if one go by Carlisle (or
rather, I suppose, it is directly in the way),
or even if one go by Liverpool, but I rather
think he will make for Newcastle this time;
to which place we have a steamboat direct.
This is a good season for steamboats, and a
bad one for coaches; for with latter, indeed,
what good season is there? Nothing in
the world is frightfuller to me of the travelling rout, than a coach on a long journey.
It is easier by half to walk it with peas (at

least boiled peas) in your shoes, were not the
time so much shorter.   The Doctor looks very
well and sonsy ; he seems in good health and
well to live ; the only change is that his head
is getting a shade of grey (quite ahead of
mine, though I am six years older), which
does not mis-seem him, but looks very well.

We had a long speculation about going to
Scotland, too, but I doubt we must renounce
it.   This summer I have finished my second
volume, but there is still the third to do, and
I must have such a tussle with it !   All summer I will struggle and wrestle, but then
about the time of the gathering in of sheaves
I too shall be gathering in.   Jane has gone
out to " buy a cotton gown," for the weather
is, at last, beautiful and warm.   Before going
she bade me send you both her best wishes
and regards, prayers for a happy pilgrimage
together.   She has been but poorly for a
good while (indeed, all the world is sick with
these east winds and perpetual changes), but
will probably be better now.

Jack and I, too, have both had our colds.
Then Anne Cook fell sick, almost danger-
ously sick for the time ; but Jack was there
and gave abundant medical help ; so the poor
creature is on her feet again, and a great

trouble of confusion is rolled out of doors thereby.

I am writing to our Mother this day. I have heard nothing from that quarter since the letter that informed me the poor little child was dead. Jean wrote part of it herself, and seemed in a very composed state, keeping her natural sorrow courageously down. Our Mother, I believe, continues there till Jean be ill again, and we hope happily well. Whether there be a frank procurable to-day I know not, but I will try. At worst I will not wait, lest you grow impatient again and get short. If you knew what a fizz I am kept in with one thing and another! Write to me when you have time to fill a sheet, — news, descriptions of how you get on, what you suffer and enjoy, what you do: these are the best. I will answer. Send an old newspaper from time to time, with two strokes on it, if you are well. Promise, however, to write instantly if you are ill. Then shall we know to keep ourselves in peace.

Farewell, dear little Sister. Give our love to our new Brother. Tell him to walk wisely and be a credit to your choice. God be with you both.

T. CARLYLE.

In Carlyle's Journal for June 1 occur these words : —

"An eternity of life were not endurable to any mortal. To me the thought of it were madness even for one day. Oh! I am far astray, wandering, lost, ' dyeing the thirsty desert with my blood in every footprint.' Perhaps God and His providence will be better to me than I hope. Peace, peace! words are idler than idle.

"I have seen Wordsworth again. I have seen Landor, Americans, Frenchman-Cavaignac the Republican. Be no word written of them. Bubble bubble, toil and trouble. I find emptiness and chagrin, look for nothing else, and on the whole can reverence no existing man, and shall do well to pity all, myself first, — or rather, last. To work, therefore. That will still me a little, if aught will."

Presently the household purse became so shrunken that the Revolution had to be dropped for two weeks, while Carlyle wrote the article on Mirabeau. This — printed first in Mill's Review, and afterward in the Miscellanies — brought in about fifty pounds. Mrs. Carlyle, meanwhile, became so ill that it was arranged for her to go home to her mother. The voyage part of the plan, — by steamer from Liverpool to Annan, — which had been merely for economy, was not carried out. Mrs. Carlyle's Liverpool uncle, John Welsh, paid her fare in the coach to Dumfries, and gave her a handsome shawl as a present for her birthday, the 14th of July.

III. CARLYLE TO MRS. HANNING, MANCHESTER.

CHELSEA, 8*th July*, Friday, 1836.

DEAR JENNY, — I write you a few words in the greatest haste, with a worthy Mr. Gibson even talking to me all the while; but I *must* write, for there is not a post to lose, and I think the news will not be unwelcome to you.

Jane is getting ill again in this fiercely hot weather, and I have persuaded her to go home for a month to her mother. She is going by Manchester, and you. Off some time to-morrow (Saturday), and will be in your town, we calculate, on Sunday, and hopes to sleep in your house that night. *This* is the news. Now we know not as yet by what coach she will come, or at what hour and what Inn she will arrive, but this Mr. Gibson, who has undertaken to go out and search over the city for the suitablest vehicle, and to engage a

seat in that for her, will take this letter in his
pocket. He, having engaged the seat, will
mark the name of it on the outside (where
see). I judge farther that this letter will
reach you on Saturday evening or next morning soon, so that there will be time. The
rest you will know how to do without telling.
I think Robert, if he be not altered from what
he was, will succeed in meeting the tired way-
farer as she steps out, which will be a great
comfort to her. She calculates on being at
full liberty to sit silent with you, or to sit
talking, to lie down on the bed, to do whatsoever she likes best to do, and to be in all
senses at home as in her own home. There
are few houses in England that could do as
much for her. I think she would like best
to be — " well let alone."

Next day, or when once right rested, Robert will conduct her to the Liverpool Railway,
and give her his " Luck by the road ;" after
which she has but a little whirl, a little sail,
— by the force of steam both ways, — and is
at Templand or Annan. She will tell you all
our news and get all yours, so I need not add
another word. Did you get a frank that I
sent you some months ago? Did you ever
send even a newspaper since? Jane has half

a thought that she may find the Doctor and
our mother with you. All good wishes to
your Goodman.

Yours, my dear Jenny, affectionately,

T. CARLYLE.

IV. TO MRS. HANNING, MANCHESTER, FROM HER
MOTHER, IN SCOTSBRIG.

November 3, 1836.

DEAR JENNY,—I have long had a mind
to write you, but have put off, as you see, till
now, and though I have nothing worth while
to say but to tell you of my welfare, which I
know you are still glad to hear. I have been
very well since you left me, though I have
taken no medicine of any kind. You will
be ready to say, "What have you been doing
all this time?" I have been very throng in
my own way. I have spun a little web of
droget and done many odd things.

We have got another fine little boy here
last Monday morning. Isabella is doing well.

They have had a long and sore fight with
the harvest. It is nearly finished. It is a
good crop, and upon the whole no great damage is done. We had a bitter snow and frost
last week; it is gone again, however, but the
weather is still coarse, with good days among.

I had a long letter from London about the time I got yours with the socks, which are very comfortable indeed. I have them on at this moment, and my feet are as warm as pie. Many thanks to the giver. The iron is likewise an excellent one, a perfect conceit. Many, many thanks.

I was sorry to hear of your lassie turning out so badly. She had too much confidence. One should trust them no farther than they see. Old James of the hill is just come up for some beasts of Alick's. He talks of taking them over the water to sell them soon. So you will perhaps have a visit of him soon.

You must not be long in writing to me, my good bairn, and tell me how you are coming on. Are you anything healthy now? I intend visiting you, if I be well. Afterward it will be the next year before I think of coming. They were all well at London when I got their letter. John was at Geneva. I long to hear from him, and to know where he is now. I am expecting word daily. The rest are all well, for aught I know; but Jamie is at Annan to-day, and he will hear of them all, as Alick was at Dumfries yesterday.

Your folk are all well. I saw William Hanning last week at the market with John. He told me he had sent away a letter that day, I think, to you. I forgot to tell you how Tom is getting on with his book. He intends going to press about New Year's Day. It will be a fine time for him. May we all go on in the strength of God, the Lord, making mention of His righteousness, even of His only, trusting in Him for all we need for time and for eternity. I had done, but have just got a letter from the good Doctor, wrote about a fortnight since. If he is well, he is near Rome by this time.

Write, for I can write none. Send me a long letter. No more.

From your own mother,
M. A. CARLYLE.

They are all well at Annan and Dumfries.

Friday. I believe Alick goes off for Liverpool to-day. Send me word when to come over, and write soon.

By the end of October, 1836, Carlyle was already wondering what he should do after finishing The French Revolution, and wrote to his brother John : " Here, with only literature for shelter, there is, I think, no continuance. Better to take a stick in your hand, and roam the earth Teufelsdröckhish ; you will get at least a stomach to eat bread, — even that denied me here." On the evening of the 12th of January, 1837, the book was finished which raised Carlyle from obscurity — so far as the public was concerned — to an undisputed place among great writers. Though popularity did not come for many a year, fame attended him from this point onward. The French Revolution was not published, however, until June; and in the interim Carlyle's circumstances looked little more promising than before. A week after he had finished the last sentence, and handed the manuscript to his wife with a since famous and often-quoted speech, he found time and spirits to send prescriptions of cheerfulness to Mrs. Hanning. The " two strokes " of a pen on a newspaper signified to the Carlyle who received the paper that all was well with the Carlyle who sent it.

V. CARLYLE TO MRS. HANNING, MANCHESTER.

5 Cheyne Row, Chelsea, London,
19th Jan'y, 1837.

My dear Jenny, — It is a long time since I heard directly of you at any length, or since you heard of me. To-day, tho' I have not the best disposition or leisure, I will send you a line : there are no franks going, but the post is always going, and you will think a shilling might be worse spent.

We are very sorry, and not without our anxieties, at the short notice Robert sent us on the Newspaper; however, the next week brought confirmation on the favourable side, and I persuade myself to hope that all is getting round again to the right state. Your health is evidently not strong; but you are growing in years, and have naturally a sound constitution; you must learn to take care and precautions, especially in the life you are now entered upon, in that huge den of reek and Cotton-fuz, where one cannot go on as in the free atmosphere of the Country. Exercise, especially exercise out of doors when it is convenient, is the best of all appliances. Do not sit motionless within doors, if there is a sun shining without, and you are able to stir. Particularly endeavour to keep a *good heart*, and avoid all moping and musing, whatever takes away your cheerfulness. Sunshine in the *inside* of one is even more important than sunshine without.

I do not understand your way of life so well as to know whether the Goodman is generally at your hand; in that case, you have both a duty to do, and society in the doing of it independently of others; but, at all events, frank communication with one's fellow-creatures is a pleasure and a medicine which no life should be without. Be not solitary, be not idle! That is a precept of old standing. *Doing* one's duties (and all creatures have their solemn duties to do), living soberly, meekly, " walking humbly before God," one has cause to hope that it will be well with him, that he shall see good in the world. Write me a letter, full of all your concerns and considerations, when you can muster disposition. I shall always be right glad of such a message. In fine, I hope the spring weather will come and set us all up a little.

Before going farther, let me mention here that a Newspaper came to me last Monday, charged nineteen shillings and some pence! I, of course, refused it. I got a sight of it, but could not ascertain accurately from whom it was. Either Alick or your Robert, I thought, but the Post people had stamped it, and sealed it, and smeared it all over, and marked it " Written on," so that I could make little of it. The cover, I noticed, was in writing paper scored with blue lines: it strikes me it may have been the Manchester paper, after all, and no writing in it but the copper-plate on a piece of one of Robert's account papers. At all events, when any more Newspapers come, the law is that the cover be of vacant blank paper; likewise we will cease writing or marking except two strokes on the cover, lest we get into trouble by it. I refused this nineteen shillings fellow; and they will be able to make no more of it, but it will make them more watchful in future. I mean to write into Annandale to the like effect.

The Doctor sends me word out of Rome that he wants a Dumfries Herald forwarded to him thither. I have not yet arranged that; but I am thinking of having this Herald (if the days answer) sent by Manchester, thro' your hands. I think it would reach you on Saturday. You could look at it, and send it on, the same day, whereby no time at all would be lost. The two strokes would always be a satisfaction. We shall see how it answers. If any such Herald, then, come your way, you know what to do with it.

It is several weeks since I had any direct tidings out of Scotland, except what James Aitken's address of the Courier gives me: it

had the sign of well-being on it last week.   I
am to write thither shortly, having a letter
of the Doctor's lying here, as I have hinted.
The Doctor says he had written a few days
before to our Mother, which has made me less
anxious about speed with this to her.   He is
well and doing tolerably well, — getting what
Practice in Rome a beginner can expect.
The Cholera was about gone from Naples,
and the panic of it from Rome, so that more
English were coming in, and he hoped to do
still better.   You can send this news into the
Scotch side when you have opportunity.

All people here have got a thing they call
Influenza, a dirty, feverish kind of cold; very
miserable, and so general as was hardly ever
seen.   Printing-offices, Manufactories, Tailor-
shops, and such like are struck silent, every
second man lying *swiftering* in his respective
place of abode.   The same seems to be the
rule in the North, too.   I suppose the miserable temperate of climate may be the cause.
Worse weather never fell from the Lift, to
my judgment, than we have here.   Reek,
mist, cold, wet; the day before yesterday
there was one of our completest London fogs,
— a thing of which I suppose you even at
Manchester can form no kind of notion.   For

we are exactly *ten times* as big as you are, and parts of us are hardly less reeky and dirty; farther, we lie *flat*, on the edge of a broad river: and now suppose there were a *mist*, black enough, and such that no smoke or emanation could rise from us, but fell again the instant it had got out of the chimney-head! People have to light candles at noon, coaches have torch-bearers running at the horses' heads. It is like a sea of ink. I wonder the people do not all drop down dead in it, — since they are not *fishes*, of a particular sort. It is cause enough for Influenza. Poor Jane, who misses nothing, has caught fast hold of this Sunday last, and has really been miserably ill. She gets better these last two days, but is weak as water; indeed, the headache at one time was quite wretched. She has been, on the whole, stronger since you saw her, but is not at all strong. As for myself, I have felt these wretched fogs penetrating into me, with a clear design to produce cough; but I have set my face against it and said No. This really does a great deal, and has served me hitherto. I hope to escape the Influenza; they say it is abating.

The Book is *done*, about a week ago: this

is my best news. I have got the first *printed* sheet, since I sat down to write this. We shall go on swiftly, it is to be hoped, and have it finished and forth into the world, say, before the month of March end. I care little what becomes of it then; it has been a sore Book to me. There are two things I was printing lately, which I would send to you, but there is no conveyance. I fear you would do little good with them, at any rate; not five shillings' worth of good, which they would cost you. Besides, if Robert or you want to see them, you can let him go to a Circulating Library and ask for the *last Number of the London and Westminster Review*. In it he will find a thing called Memoirs of Mirabeau: that thing is mine. The other thing is in Fraser's Magazine, — half of it; the other half will be in the February Number: it is called Diamond Necklace.

This latter was written at Craigenputtock a good while ago. I see your Manchester Editor feels himself aggrieved by it, worthy man, but hints that there may be some mistake on *his* part; which I do very seriously assure him is my opinion, too. Other Editors, it would seem, sing to the same tune.

After this Book is printed, it remains uncertain what I shall do next. One thing I am firmly enough resolved on : not to spend the summer *here*. I will have myself rested, and see the fields green and the sky blue yet one year, follow what may. Many things call me towards Scotland ; but nothing can yet be determined upon. If I go Northward, Manchester is a likely enough step for me ; nay, perhaps the Doctor may be home from Rome, and we shall both be there ! Nothing is yet fixed ; we will hope all this.

And now, my dear Sister, I must bid thee good day. Salute Robert from me with all manner of good wishes. I have known him as a " fell fellow " since he was hardly longer than my leg. Tell him to be diligent in business, and also (for that is another indispensable thing) fervent in spirit, struggling to serve *God*. Make thou a good wife to him, helping him in all right things by counsel and act. Good be with you both ! Jane sends you all good wishes from her sick bed, and " was grieved to hear of what had happened you." She will be better in a day or two.

Your affectionate Brother,
T. CARLYLE.

The next letter, "a holy and a cheerful
note" from Margaret Carlyle to her daughter,
falls of necessity between 1836 and 1840, the
year of Mrs. Hanning's going to Manchester
and that of her leaving it. The statement
that "Tom . . . has to begin to lecture the
first of May, and has no time to prepare,"
points to 1837; for all the following courses
Carlyle had time to make ready. This first
series, with German Literature for subject,
was suddenly arranged by a number of Carlyle's friends, — Miss Martineau zealous among
them, — in the fear that, unless things bright-
ened for him, he would be forced to leave
London, "and perhaps England." The lectures were a great success; Carlyle *spoke*,
instead of *reading*, to "an audience of Mar-
chionesses, Ambassadors, ah me! and what
not;" and the resulting sum of one hundred and thirty-five pounds, with the promise
of another course for the next season, settled the household gods more firmly on their
pedestals. In the words of Mrs. Carlyle,
"Nothing that he has ever tried seems to
me to have carried such conviction to the
public heart that he is a real man of genius, and worth being kept alive at a moderate
rate."

VI. TO MRS. HANNING, MANCHESTER, FROM HER
MOTHER.

Scotsbrig, *April 9th* [1837].

DEAR JENNY,—I have nothing worth writing at this time. We are all in our usual health. I have had little Grace with me these three weeks. Now I have to go to Dumfries this week to put some money in the bank for John, your brother. It is at Dumfries by this time. I told Mary to bid you write me soon and tell me how you are coming on. If you have not written, write to Dumfries. Do you know that Jane has been very badly? She is rather better. Thank God, her mother is there with them. She took a coach and went straight for London. Tom is in a great hubble at this time: you will know he has to begin to lecture the first of May, and has no time to prepare. May God be with him and all of us, and as our day is so may our strength be, and may He prepare us for whatever He see meet to come in our way, that it may be for His glory and our good in the end. Our time is short at longest: may we have grace given us to improve it.

I had no thought of writing at this time,

but Fanny Caruthers called and told me she was going to Manchester. She is much altered: I did not know her. Now, Jenny, I intend to see you this summer; I cannot say when, but if health permit I will come. If I am long in coming, I can stay the longer: it depends on Tom when he comes home. It will be June at the soonest before he can get away. I had a letter from him shortly which troubled me not a little, telling of Jane's illness. She is rather better, but still confined to her bed at last accounts, which was about a week ago. I had a letter of John: he was well then. Write soon and tell me how you keep your health, now this cold weather is come, and how is Robert. Thank him in my name for nursing you so well when you were poorly. I hope you are stout now. Take good care of yourself and be well when I come over. I long to see you both. I will add no more, but am still

Your loving mother,
MARGARET A. CARLYLE.

God be with us all, and bless us, and do us good.

Clap your thumbs on mistakes.

On the 7th of June Carlyle wrote to Ster-

ling, "I cannot say a word to you of the
book or of the lectures, except that by the
unspeakable blessing of Heaven they are finished."   "A few days after the date of this
letter," says Froude, "Carlyle fled to Scotland, fairly broken down."   That he lingered
a fortnight longer in Chelsea, however, the
following letter is witness.

VII. CARLYLE TO MRS. HANNING, MANCHESTER.

5 CHEYNE ROW, CHELSEA, LONDON.
20th June, 1837.

MY DEAR JENNY, — I write to-day with
one of the worst of pens and in the extreme
hurry of packing, to say that I am just coming off for Annandale, and shall take Lan-
cashire in my way.   I think of taking the
steamboat to-morrow morning for Hull.   After that, I believe we go by Leeds and then
to Manchester, where I hope to find you and
your Goodman well.   The times and the distances after getting to Hull, as we hope on
Thursday, are unknown to me.   Most probably, I should think, it will be on Saturday
that I get to you, but it may be the day after,
it may be the day before, for all is yet uncertain; nay, there is a certain Dr. Hunter
in Leeds, a cousin of Jane's, with whom I

may (though that is not very likely) loiter an
hour or two. We shall see. We shall hope
to meet all in order some how or other at
last.

Jane is to stay here till I come back, her
mother keeping her company. Jane, as you
perhaps know, has been very ill. She has
now grown much stronger again, but still not
strong enough. Her mother hastily joined
us when things were at the worst in the
month of April, and will not quit us till we
get together again.

I am not very eminently well at present,
yet neither is anything special gone wrong
with me. I want rest, and mean to have that
now at Scotsbrig. I have got my book completely done. I gave a course of lectures
too, &c., &c., and have " got all by " for the
present. I seem to myself to require a little
while of repose as the one thing needful.

A newspaper came the other day from the
Doctor, indicating that he was well. He is
not in Rome through the Summer, but in a
place called Albano, not far from Rome. He
seemed to consider it as not unlikely that he
might be here in September again. He had
succeeded pretty well at Rome as a Practi-
tioner.

Last time I heard from Annandale our Mother and all the rest were well. It is not very long since, — some three weeks or little more. They also reported well of you at Manchester.

Give my compliments to Robert. Say I mean to ask his assistance in buying a quantity of *breeches*, as I pass through that huge Weaving-shop of the World. I ought to get them there better than elsewhere.

Let us hope, therefore, that on Saturday, or some time near before or near after that day, I shall succeed in finding you at Bank Street and finding all right.

I have not a moment's time more. Indeed, what more is there to be said at present with such a pen?

I remain always, my dear sister,
Your affectionate
T. CARLYLE.

James Carlyle was now with his mother, farming Scotsbrig for her. Alick did afterward go to America, and died there. "John of Cockermouth" was a half-brother. "James Austin and Mary" are Carlyle's brother-in-law and sister.

VIII. CARLYLE TO MRS. HANNING, MANCHESTER.

Scotsbrig, 18th July, 1837.

My dear Jenny, — According to promise,
I set about writing you a word of Scotch
news, now that I am fairly settled here and
know how things are. The railway train
whirled me away from you rapidly that evening. Next evening, about the same hour, we
were getting out of Liverpool harbour, and
on the following morning, between seven and
eight o'clock, I had got my eye upon Alick
waving to me from the end of the Jetty at
Annan. It is almost three weeks now that
I have been here and found all well, but it
was only the day before yesterday that we
got our first visit to Dumfries made out, and
could rightly report about matters there. I
fancied a newspaper with two strokes would
communicate the substance of what was to be
said in the interim.

There has been a good deal of discussion
about Alick and his going to America. He
himself seemed of mind to go, but not
very strongly or hopefully set on it. Our
Mother, again, was resolute against it, and
made such a lamenting as was sufficient to
dishearten one more inclined than he. So

now I think it seems fixed so far as that he *will not go.* What he is to do here one does not so well see, but it will evidently be a great point gained for him that he give up thinking about departure, and direct his whole industry to ascertaining how he can manage here where he is. Men of far less wit than he do contrive to manage, when once they have set their heart on it. Jamie is quite ready to go to Puttock and give up Scotsbrig to him, but I still rather think there will nothing come of that; nay, some think Alick himself does not at bottom wish that, but is satisfied with finding Jamie so far ready to accommodate him and keep him at home. He seems very tranquil, cheerfuller than he was and altogether steady; likelier to have a little fair luck than he was a while ago. He must persist where he is. There is nothing that can prosper without perseverance. Perseverance will make many a thing turn out well that looked ill enough once. John of Cockermouth is gone off to America about a fortnight ago with all his family. I got him a letter from Burnswark to a brother of his at New York. I doubt not he will do well. Clow of Land has his property advertised for sale; means to be off about the end of August, which also

I reckon prudent. With two or three thousand pounds in his pocket and four or five strong sons at his back, a man may make a figure in America. James Austin and Mary were at one time talking of America, but they also have given it up.

We had a letter from the Doctor shortly after my arrival here. He is well, living at Albano, a summer residence some twenty miles from Rome. He speaks of it being possible, or probable, that he may get back to England in September, but it is not certain. He will be pretty sure to come by Manchester and you if he come Northward. The rest, as I have already hinted, are all well and following their usual course. Jamie and his wife and two sons go along very briskly. His crops look well. He had his Peat-stack up (and mother's little one beside it) and his hay mown, though the late rains and thunder have retarded that a little. The country never looked beautifuller in my remembrance, green and leafy; the air is fresh, and all things smiling and rejoicing and growing. Austin is busy enough now with work. He had a bad time of it in spring, when horse provender was so dear. The children are well, — even the eldest looks better than I expected,

— and Mary, their mother, seems hearty and thrifty. I mentioned that we had been at Dumfries. Alick took up our Mother and me on Friday last in a rough "Dandycart" of Mrs. Scott's with a beast of Jamie's. One of the first questions my Mother asked of Jean was, "Hast thou had any word from Jenny?" To which the answer was "No." Jean's child is running about quite brisk, though a little thinner than it once was; from teeth, I suppose. James Aitken has plenty of work, three or four journeymen. In short, they seem doing well. Finally, Jamie (Maister Cairlill) authorizes me to report that he this day met with a brother of thy Robert's, who said that the Peat-knowes too were all well. The day after my arrival here I fell in with William Hanning, the father, on Middlebie Brae, measuring some Dykes, I think, with a son of Pottsfowns. He looked as well as I have seen him do. The same man as ever, though he must be much older than he once was. The tea parcel was forwarded to him, or sent for, by my desire, that same night.

Our good Mother here is quite well in health; indeed, as well every way as one could expect, though doubtless she is a little

lonelier now than when you were with her.
She complains of nothing, but does her endeavour to make the best of all things. She
wishes you "to write very soon and tell her
how the world is serving you." She would
have sent a word or two to that effect in her
own hand, she says, but "having a good
clerk" (me, namely) "she does not need." I
am to confirm her promise of coming with
me when I return southward, and staying till
you tire of her. There was word from Jane
on Sunday gone a week. She wrote in haste,
but at great length, and seemed very cheerful. She will not come hither this time, I
think. Her mother is to return home about
the end of this month. Jane appears quite
prepared to stay by herself. She has some
friends yonder whom she is much with, and
she rather likes the treat. Mrs. Welsh expects Liverpool people with her to Templand,
and can stay no longer.

I have ended my paper, dear Jenny, and
given one of the meagrest outlines of our
news. You will see, however, that nothing
is going wrong with us; that we are thinking
of you and desirous to hear from you. Be a
good bairn and a good wife, and help your
Goodman faithfully in all honest things. He

is a thrifty fellow with a good whole heart.
There is no danger of him. Help one another. Be good to one another. God's blessing with you both. All here salute you.

I am always

Your affectionate brother,

T. CARLYLE.

Meantime, while Jamie was building his
peat-stack in "the beautifullest weather" that
Carlyle had ever seen, Alick was setting up a
shop in the village of Ecclefechan, and The
French Revolution was beginning to take the
English-reading world for its parish. The
French verdict was for the most part adverse.
Mérimée, whether or not he agreed with the
translators in describing Carlyle as *le phéno-
mène d'un protestant poétique*, expressed a
sincere desire to throw the writer out of the
window. But Dickens carried the book about
with him, Southey read it six times running,
and Mill, approving his opposite, maintained
that the much berated style was of high ex-
cellence. Carlyle, wishing to "lie vacant,"
neither read nor so much as saw many of the
reviews, though he heard of most of them.
One untactful friend sent him the opinion
of a certain critical journal, with which he

forthwith "boiled his teakettle."　Much more than a pot-boiler was one enthusiastic review, although that function of his article was sadly important to the writer, for whom Vanity Fair and fame were still ten years ahead. Writes Carlyle to his brother : " I understand there have been many reviews of a very mixed character.　I got one in the Times last week. The writer is one Thackeray, a half-monstrous Cornish giant, kind of painter, Cambridge man, and Paris newspaper correspondent, who is now writing for his life in London.　I have seen him at the Bullers' and at Sterling's. His article is rather like him, and I suppose calculated to do the book good."

One adds involuntarily : —

> " Brigadier, répondit Pandore,
> Brigadier, vous avez raison."

Without regard to reviewers, and in spite of the cholera, the homely idyl goes melodiously on. "Jean and her two Jamies" are Carlyle's sister, Mrs. Aitken, her husband and little son.　"Jamie of Scotsbrig" is, of course, Carlyle's brother. Betty Smail's short history may be found in Froude's First Forty Years of Carlyle, vol. i. p. 119.

IX. CARLYLE TO MRS. HANNING, MANCHESTER.

SCOTSBRIG, ECCLEFECHAN,
28 *Aug.* 1837.

DEAR JENNY, — Your letter to Mary at
Annan got this length on Saturday night.
As you appear to be impatient for news from
this quarter, not unreasonably, having had
none for six weeks, I am appointed to write
you a few lines without any loss of time whatever, — a thing I can easily enough do, being
even idler to-day than common.

We were not so well pleased to hear of
your fecklessness and pain in the stomach
during the last fortnight, but we hope it is
but something derived from the season and
will not continue. There is very often a kind
of " British Cholera " in this harvest time. It
is even very frequent at present in this region, owing partly to the air (as they say),
and chiefly, perhaps, to the new potatoes and
other imperfectly ripened substances which
people eat. Jamie, here, had a cast of it for
two days just a week ago, rather sharp, but
he is free now. Our Mother too was taken
with it, — came home rather ill from Ecclefechan one day, — but by aid of Castor and
some prime Brandy has got quite round

again. You do not say that the disorder has got that length with you, but very probably it is something related to the same business. The only remedy is to be careful of what one eats, to take due moderate exercise in the open air, in case of extremity employing a little medicine. Cold, especially cold feet are very bad ; but the great thing is to take care of one's self, especially to take care what one eats. New potatoes are very unwholesome for some people.

We are now all well here, and with the slight exception mentioned above have been so ever since I wrote last. Alick brought us news of you. Alick's news are the main ones I have now to send you. He quitted Annan on Monday last (this day gone a week), and has been in the Big house at Ecclefechan ever since. I suppose he explained to you and Robert the plan he had of setting up a shop there. He has gathered himself together, and is all alive after that same enterprise now. We had him and little Tom over here all yesterday. Mother, Jamie, and I walked with them to Cleughbrae in the evening. To-day, as we understand, he has got masons and actually broken in upon the house to repair it and arrange it for that

object; Hale Moffet and his retinue having
been got out. It is in a sad state of wreck,
the poor house, but Alick expects to put a
new face on it with great despatch indeed;
and then, " shop drawers " and all the rest
being provided, and James Aitken's brush
having given the last touch to it, he will un-
fold his wares and try the thing in the name
of Hope. We all pray heartily that it may
prosper beyond his expectations. Ecclefechan is a sad Village : only last Friday night
some blackguard broke 14 panes of the Meeting House windows. Fancy such an act of
dastardly atrocity as that ! But it lies in the
centre of a tolerable country, too, and certain
there is *need* of some good shop and honest
Trader there.

I have seen Mary pretty frequently, the
last time on Friday last. She is very well,
and all her bairns are well. James has always some work, though seldom enough, and
Mary is the brightest, thriftiest little creature
that can be. They go on there as well as
one could hope in these times. We had a
letter from the Doctor, too : still in the same
place, — Albano, near Rome ; still well ; uncertain as to his future movements or engage-
ments, though it must be settled some way

before this date, if we knew how. He seemed to think it very unlikely that he would be here in the present autumn, the likeliest of all that he would try to return next spring. The Cholera was in that country, but had not got to them. We fancy they will not fail to fly out of the road of it, if it advance too near.

I was at Dumfries since I wrote: up to Templand, and then again at Dumfries on my return. Mrs. Welsh came home several weeks ago, and had at the time I was up, and has still, her Liverpool friends with her. The house was very crowded. I was not very well, and stayed only four and twenty hours or so, cutting out my way in spite of all entreaties. Jean and her two Jamies are very tolerably well : the elder Jamie a thrifty, effectual, busy man ; the younger as yet altogether silent, staggering and tripping about, — one of the *gleggest* little elves I have seen. There is talk of her coming down to Annan this very week to have the benefit of the tide for sea bathing. Jamie of Scotsbrig, who goes up to-morrow to pay his rent, will bring us word.

The other morning, walking out, I met Robert's father at the " Lengland's Nett,"

coming down from Dairlaw Hills with a row
of bog-hay carts he had been buying at Dairlaw Hills. He was hale and well to look at,
and reported all well. I suppose he has been
very busy of late; seldom were so many
roups seen in one season; all the farmers
selling off, none of them having money for
their rent day; Land farm, and now all the
stock, crop, and household furniture have
been sold off. Poor Clow goes off for America on Wednesday morning by the Liverpool
steamer. People are all sorry. The Burn-
foot Irvings, or Sandy Cowie for them, have
bought his land : £4000.

Betty Smail, bound for Ecclefechan, has
been waiting this half hour till I should be
done; I did not know of her when I began.
The needfullest thing, therefore, that I can
do is to tell you about our coming. It will
be soon, but is still uncertain when. I
should say in about a fortnight, — nay, in a
day or so *less ;* but it depends somewhat on
a letter we look for from Jane which has not
yet come to hand. Jane, you must know,
after her mother's departure went into the
country with the Sterlings, friends of hers.
I wish her to stay there while she likes, and
would get home about the same time as she;

a month was the time she first spoke of, and
that I have little doubt will suffice, — so my
guess is as above given. A newspaper with
one stroke on it will come to you (barring
mistakes) two days before you are to look for
us. This shall be a token, and we need not
write any more. Alick has some talk of
coming with us to get his goods ready *then*,
but I think *he* will hardly be ready. The
butter and another firkin of butter has been
talked of and will be forthcoming, but it
seems dubious whether any of it will get with
us. It can come before or after, I believe
safe and with little expense. Mother will
bring "some pounds of it" in her box. I
shall perhaps be obliged to go back by Liverpool, and must not calculate to stay more
with you than a day. My Mother sends you
both her love (she is smoking here); she
" will tell you all her news " when we come.
Compliments and good wishes to Robert from
all of us. We are glad to hear his trade is
better. A glegg fellow like him will get
through worse troubles than this. God keep
you, my dear little Jenny.

Your affectionate Brother,

T. CARLYLE.

X. TO MRS. HANNING, MANCHESTER, FROM HER MOTHER.

[SCOTSBRIG] *January* 11*th* [1838].

DEAR CHILDREN, — I received your letter this day about mid-day. Then Alick and his family came here, so we talked on till bed-time ; and now they are gone to bed. I am sorry to hear that Jenny is poorly. I intend to see you very soon ; I cannot say pointedly which day yet. I am going down to Annan with Alick, and will fix. It shall not be long, God willing. I have some thoughts of taking the steamer. Keep up your heart, Jenny, and be well when I come. Trust in God, casting all your cares on Him. He is a kind father to all them that put their trust in Him. I will say no more to-night; it is late. Do you think the railway is passable ?

I had not finished this scrawl when I received your last letter, of which I was very glad. It is all well, God's will be done. I was coming by the steamer on Thursday or Friday. Now I will let the storm blow by. Now, Jenny, be very careful of yourself; take care of cold, and likewise what you eat. May God's blessing rest on us all. May He make us thankful for all His ways of dealing with us. Write soon. You may direct to Annan, as I will be there some time. Could you let Tom know that I am there, also, and that I am well? Now, bairns, write soon. You see I cannot write, though nobody would take greater pleasure in it.

Your own mother,

MARGARET A. C.

P. S. My tooth is better, though not very sound yet. I forgot to thank you very kindly for the things you sent me.

In the two ensuing years Carlyle gave two more courses of lectures, both notably successful. Among many other new acquaintances was Mr. Baring, afterward Lord Ashburton, who, with his two wives, was to figure so largely in the lives of Carlyle and his wife. Sartor Resartus was published in England, and republished in the United States. Chartism was written and printed. Other events of the same biennium were Mrs. Carlyle's " only Soirée," the appearance of Count d'Orsay in Cheyne Row, and Mr. Marshall's gift to Carlyle of a mare, — " Citoyenne " to be called.

After several visits in Scotland during the summer of 1838, Carlyle went home again to Scotsbrig. On his return thence, he spent a few days in Manchester with Mrs. Hanning. "He had been put to sleep in an old bed, which he remembered in his father's house." "I was just closing my senses in sweet oblivion," wrote he, "when the watchman, with a voice like the deepest groan of the Highland bagpipe, or what an ostrich corncraik might utter, groaned out Groo-o-o-o close under me, and set me all in a gallop again. Groo-o-o-o ; for there was no articulate announcement at all in it, that I could gather. Groo-o-o-o, repeated again and again at various distances, dying out and then growing loud again, for an hour or more. I grew impatient, bolted out of bed, flung up the window. Groo-o-o-o. There he was advancing, lantern in hand, a few yards off me. 'Can't you give up that noise?' I hastily addressed him. 'You are keeping a person awake. What good is it to go howling and groaning all night, and deprive people of their sleep?' He ceased from that time — at least I heard no more of him. No watchman, I think, has been more astonished for some time back. At five in the morning all was as still as sleep and darkness. At half past five all went off like an enormous mill-race or ocean-tide. The Boom-m-m, far and wide. It was the mills that were all starting then, and creishy drudges by the million taking post there. I have heard few sounds more impressive to me in the mood I was in."

The following letter belongs to the time between the Hannings' departure from Manchester and Mr. Hanning's sailing for America. Kirtlebridge, where they were now living, is a few miles southeast of Ecclefechan. " The little ' trader,' " the " bit creeture," was probably Mrs. Hanning's first child, Margaret Aitken Carlyle, who was not yet two years old. The reference to the new penny post marks an era.

XI.   CARLYLE TO MRS. HANNING, KIRTLEBRIDGE.

5 Cheyne Row, Chelsea, London,
7 *Feb.* 1840.

DEAR JENNY, — Had I known definitely how to address a word to you, I might surely have done so long before this. We have heard in general that you are stationed somewhere in the Village of Kirtlebridge or near it, and we fancy in general that your husband is struggling along with his old impetuosity. From yourself we have no tidings.

Pray, now that the Postage is so cheap, send us a pennyworth some day. I address this through Alick, fancying such may be the best way.

I enclose my last letter from the Doctor. I wrote to him the day before yesterday to his final destination. I calculate he may have got my letter to-day, — that is two days after his arrival. By that note all seems to be going well with him ; — we are all well here, as well as our wont is, and fighting along with printers, proof sheets &c, &c. Jane cannot regularly get out ; so horribly tempestuous, wet and uncertain is the weather, which keeps her still sickly, but she never breaks actually down. How is the little " trader," as Jean or some of them call her ? I remember the "bit creeture" very distinctly.

This is the worst year or among the worst for working people ever seen in man's memory. Robert must not take this as a measure of his future success, but toil away steadfastly in sure hope of *better* times. It is well anyway that you are out of Manchester ; nothing there but hunger, contention and despair — added to the reek and dirt ! Be diligent and fear nothing.

Do you often run over to see our dear Mother in her Upper Room yonder? It will be a great comfort to her that she has you so near. Pray explain to me what part of the Village it is that you live in. I thought I knew it all, but I do not know Firpark Nook. Give my best wishes to your Goodman. Accept my thanks for your written remembrance, from one who always silently remembers you in his heart.

On April 23 of this year Carlyle wrote in his journal, "Miscellanies out, and Chartism second thousand." A month later he relieved his mother's anxiety about the last of his lectures on Heroes and Hero-Worship: "I contrived to tell them something about poor Cromwell, and I think to convince them that he was a great and true man, the valiant soldier in England of what John Knox had preached in Scotland. In a word, the people seemed agreed that it was my best course of lectures, this." Certainly his *last* course of lectures, this. He never spoke from a platform again till twenty-six years later, when, as Lord Rector, he addressed the students of Edinburgh University. He detested the "mixture of prophecy and play-acting." In

CARLYLE IN THE GARDEN OF 5 CHEYNE ROW, CHELSEA

July 20, 1857

the midst of his own work of making ready
these final lectures for publication, Carlyle
found time to push the London Library
along. He thought England, as regarded its
provision of books for the poor, in "a condition worthier of Dahomey than of England."

Yet, in spite of this good and successful
work for the library, Carlyle was of a mind
to write, on July 3 : "Alas ! I get so dyspep-
tical, melancholic, half mad in the London
summer : all courage to do anything but hold
my peace fades away ; I dwindle into the
pusillanimity of the ninth part of a tailor,
feel as if I had nothing I could do but ' die
in my hole like a poisoned rat.' " He was
apparently brought to the pitch of applying
to himself this most terrible word of Swift's
by the necessity of serving on a special jury.
Let us set over against it what he said —
never to be too often quoted — about a friend
whom he found sitting smoking in the garden
one evening, with Mrs. Carlyle : " A fine,
large - featured, dim - eyed, bronze-coloured,
shaggy-headed man is Alfred ; dusty, smoky,
free and easy, who swims outwardly and
inwardly with great composure in an inarticulate element of tranquil chaos and tobacco

smoke. Great now and then when he does emerge, — a most restful, brotherly, solid-hearted man." Taken together with what Tennyson himself called " the dirty monk " portrait, this probably gives a better picture of him than most of us could have made for ourselves with the eye of the flesh. Other, less welcome visitors came to Carlyle that summer, — among them a young woman from Boston, whom he called " a diseased rosebud." But America sent money as well as flowers, and the summer, according to Froude, brought the net result up to four hundred pounds.

By August, the lecture-writing now two thirds done, Carlyle, having so far taken no holiday, made a week's riding-tour in Sussex on the back of the gift-horse, Citoyenne. " Mrs. Carlyle described to us, some years after," says " the skilful biographer," " in her husband's presence, his setting out on this expedition ; she drew him in her finest style of mockery, — his cloak, his knapsack, his broad-brimmed hat, his preparation of pipes, etc., — comparing him to Dr. Syntax. He laughed as loud as any of us, — it was impossible not to laugh ; but it struck me, even then, that the wit, however brilliant, was rather untender."

On the eve of riding forth, Carlyle wrote to his mother. The Bullers, mentioned in the letter which follows, were the family of Charles Buller, to whom he had been tutor. Buller died eight years afterward, in the midst of a brilliant parliamentary career. The " clergyman " was probably the Rev. Julius Hare. I find no record of a visit to Erskine until three years later. Carlyle had written to his brother John, in the winter of 1838 : " Did you ever see Thomas Erskine, the Scotch saint? I have seen him several times lately, and like him as one would do a draught of sweet rustic mead, served in cut glasses and a silver tray ; one of the gentlest, kindliest, best bred of men. He talks greatly about 'Symbols,' and other Teufelsdröckhiana ; seems not disinclined to let the Christian religion pass for a kind of mythus, provided men can retain the spirit of it. . . . On the whole I take up with my old love for the Saints." And from that time Carlyle held much salutary communion with "St. Thomas," as Mrs. Carlyle used playfully to call him.

XII.   CARLYLE TO HIS MOTHER, SCOTSBRIG.

CHELSEA, 1st *August*, 1840.

MY DEAR MOTHER, — Before setting out
on my long-talked-of excursion I must send
you a word. I am to go to the Bullers' place
to-morrow, a place near Epsom (the great race
course) some eighteen miles of. I am to ride
out with a Macintosh before my saddle and a
small round *trunk* the size of a quartern loaf
fastened behind, and no clothes upon me that
bad weather will spoil. I shall be one of the
most original figures ! I mean to stay a day
or two about Buller's, riding to and fro to
see the fine green country. I have written
to a clergyman, an acquaintance of mine on
the South coast some 40 miles farther off : if
he repeat the invitation he once gave me,
perhaps I shall ride to him and see the place
where William the Conqueror fought &c. and
have one dip in the sea. I mean to be out
in all about a week. The weather has grown
suddenly bright. I calculate the sight of the
green earth spotted yellow with ripe corn will
do me good. After that I am to part with
my horse : the expense of it is a thing I cannot but continually grudge. I think it will
suit better henceforth to get rolled out on a

railway some 20 miles, clear of all bricks and reek, to *walk* then for half a day, now and then, and so come home at night again. The expense of a horse every day here is nearer four than three shillings, far too heavy for a little fellow like me, whom even *it* does not make altogether healthy. I have offered to give the beast to Mr. Marshall (son of the original donor), who kept her for me last winter. I hope he will accept on my return. It will be much the handsomest way of ending the concern. If he refuses I think I shall sell. I meditated long on riding all the way up to Carlisle and you! But in the humor I am in, I had not heart for it. These Southern coasts too are a still newer part of England for me. I give up the *riding* Northward, but not the *coming* Northward yet, as you shall hear.

My Fourth Lecture was finished three days ago. On returning *strong,* as I hope to do a week hence, I will attack my *two* remaining lectures and dash them off speedily. The Town will be empty — none to disturb me. About the end of August I may hope to have my hands quite free, and then! Thomas Erskine invites me to Dundee &c. There are steamers, steam coaches, — I shall surely see you.

Alick's good letter gave me welcome tidings of you. I had read your own dear little epistle before. Heaven be praised for your welfare. I am glad to hear of "the peatshed" and figure to myself the *cauldron* singing under your windows. I have written to-day to Jack. There had come a letter from Miss Elliott for him from the Isle of Wight : he once talked of settling there. I know not whether that is still in the wind again. He will have to decide about the Pellipar affair in three weeks or less.

To-day I enclose a little half sovereign. You must accept it merely to buy gooseberries : they are really very wholesome. I am to go into the City to send off some money for the Bank at Dumfries. I am in great haste. I will write again directly on my return if not sooner.

Alick's letter, tell him, was the pleasantest he has sent for many a day. I thank him much for it and will answer soon. I still owe Jamie a letter too : he is very patient, but shall be paid. Did you ever go near the sea again ? This is beautiful weather for it now. It would do you and little Tom good, I think.

Jane still likes the warmth and salutes you

all. Wish me a good journey! It is like to
be a very brief and smooth one. Adieu,
dear Mother.

Carlyle was disappointed in his hope of
going home. He did not visit Scotsbrig
again for another year.

So long before as January, 1839, Carlyle
had written to his brother : " I have my face
turned partly towards Oliver Cromwell and
the Covenant time in England and Scotland."
He continued to read and think much on the
subject; and in the autumn of 1840 he wrote
to Mr. Erskine : " I have got lately, not till
very lately, to fancy that I see in Cromwell
one of the greatest tragic souls we have ever
had in this kindred of ours." But in this
letter to his sister, as in so many another,
there is no mention save of the close family
kindred of the Carlyles : —

XIII.   CARLYLE TO MRS. HANNING, KIRTLEBRIDGE.

5 Cheyne Row, Chelsea, 7 *October,* 1840.

Dear Jenny, — Will you take a word
from me to-day in place of many hundreds
which I wish I had the means of sending
you? My time is very limited indeed, but
the sight of my handwriting may be a kind

of enlivener to your kind thoughts about me.
My dear Mother tells me you are afraid sometimes I may have forgotten you. Believe
that never, my dear little sister, it will forever
be an error if you do!   The whirl I am kept
in here is a thing you can form no notion of,
nor how natural or indeed inevitable it is for
me to give up writing letters at all except
when I am bound and obliged to do it.   You
have no lack of *news* from me ; to my Mother
at least I send abundant details.   Did I not
answer your letter too?   I surely meant and
ought to have done it.   If at any time you
wanted the smallest thing that I could do for
you, and wrote about, I should be busier than
I have ever yet been, if I did not answer. —
In short, dear Jenny, whatever sins I may
have, whatever *more* I may seem to have, try
to think handsomely of them, to forgive
them.   And above all things, consider that
whether I write many letters or few, my
affection for you is a thing that will never
leave me.

My Mother tells me frequently how good
you are to her ; what a satisfaction it is that
you are so near her.   I thank you a hundred
times for your goodness to her ; but I know
you do not need my thanks or encourage-

ment — and to me it is a real comfort to reflect that you, with your true heart and helpful hand, are always so near. Surely it is a duty for us all, and a blessing in the doing of it, to take care of our Mother, and promote her comfort by all means possible to us! I will love you better and better for this.

You would see by my Mother's last letter, where the Doctor is at present. I have heard nothing since I had a Newspaper from Dumfries, the other day, no letters. I mentioned that the box for Scotsbrig was to *be* sent off; it *went* accordingly and is now on the way to Liverpool, likely to be with you soon. There is a small parcel in it for you. We rejoice to hear that Robert prospers in his business: it is difficult to prosper in any business at present. A man of industry, sobriety, and steadiness of purpose; such a man has a chance if anybody have. Jane is certainly in better health this year than I have seen her for a good while. We wait to see what she will say to the *cold weather!* I myself am as well as usual; no great shakes of a *wellness* at any time. I expect to be busy, *very busy* this winter, which is the best consolation for all things. How I should like

to hear of Jamie's harvest being all *thatched!*
My love to my Mother, to Alick and all the
rest. Jane unites with me in special remembrances to Robert and the *glegg* little lassie.

Yours, dear Jenny, in great haste, in all
truth,   T. CARLYLE.

Late in November, Carlyle, "greatly
against wont," went out to dinner. Among
the people he met were "Pickwick" and old
Rogers, "still brisk, courteous, kindly affectionate — a good old man, pathetic to look
upon." Carlyle's acquaintances did not always grow in his favor, and six years later he
said of Rogers : " I do not remember any old
man (he is now eighty-three) whose manner
of living gave me less satisfaction." In this
winter of 1840–41, his dissatisfaction with
things in general made him think at times of
so desperate a move as retreating again to
Craigenputtock. Still he kept on with the
reading of " needful books." " He has had
it in his head for a good while," said Mrs.
Carlyle to a correspondent, on the 8th of
January, 1841, " to write a ' life of Cromwell,'
and has been sitting for months back in a
mess of great dingy folios, the very look of
which is like to give me locked-jaw."

Mrs. Hanning's second child, Mary, was born December 24, 1840.

XIV. CARLYLE TO MRS. HANNING, KIRTLEBRIDGE.

CHELSEA, 15*th January*, 1841.

DEAR JENNY, — We have heard very frequently from Alick of late about you, for which punctuality we are greatly obliged to him. You have had a bad turn, poor little Jenny, and we were all anxious enough to hear from day to day, as you may believe, how it went with you. Alick reports of late, yesterday in particular, that you are now considered out of danger, steadily getting better. We will hope and believe it so, till we hear otherwise. You must take good care of yourself. This weather is good for no creature, and must be worst of all for one in your situation. Do not venture from the fire at all, till the horrible slush of snow be off the ground.

And what becomes of our good Mother all this time ? She could not be at rest of course if she were not beside you, watching over you herself. Alick struggles to report favourably of her, but we have our own apprehensions. What can I do but again and again urge her to take all possible precautions about herself (which however she will not do!) and trust that she may escape without serious mischief. If you were once up again I will fancy *you* taking care of her. It must be a great comfort to have you so near her — within walking distance in the good season.

We have never had here so ugly a winter: first violent frost, snow &c., then still nastier times of the thawing sort; for a week past there has been nothing but sleet, rime and slobber, the streets half an inch deep with slush and yet a cake of slippery ice lying below that; so in spite of daily and hourly sweeping and scraping, they constantly continue. I, with some few others, go daily out, whatever wind blow. I am covered to the throat in warm wool of various textures and can get into heat in spite of fate. Jane too holds out wonderfully, ventures forth when there is a bright blink once in a week; sits quiet as a mouse when the winds are piping abroad. We understand you are far deeper in snow than we. I believe there is now a good thick quilt of it lying over the entire surface of the Island.

The Doctor was here till Tuesday morning. We saw him daily with much speech and satisfaction. A letter yesterday announced that

they were fairly settled in Wight again.
He looked as well as need be.

I have sent by Alick a bit half-sovereign
to buy the poor new bairn a new pock. You
must take it without grumbling. Tell my
dear Mother that she *must* take care of herself, that I will write to her before many days
go. Better health to us all. Our kind wishes
to Robert. Good be with you every one.

Your affectionate brother,
T. CARLYLE.

Here is another and a more highly elaborated bit of London weather from an undated
fragment in Mrs. Hanning's possession at the
time of her death : —

" Our weather is grown decidedly good for
the last three days; very brisk, clear and dry.
Before that it was as bad as weather at any
time need be : long continued plunges of wet,
then clammy, glarry days on days of *half*
wet (a kind of weather peculiar to London,
and fully uglier than *whole* wet) : — a world
of black sunless pluister, very unpleasant to
move about in ! The incessant travel makes
everything mud here, in spite of all that clats
and besoms can do ; a kind of mud, too,
which is as fine as paint, and actually almost

sticks like a kind of paint! I took, at last,
into the country, with old clothes and trousers
folded up; there the mud was *natural* mud,
and far less of it, indeed, *little* of it in comparison with other country. We dry again
in a single day of brisk wind."

Early in 1841 Carlyle arranged with Fraser
for the publication of Heroes and Hero-worship. "The Miscellanies, Sartor, and the
other books," says Froude, "were selling
well, and fresh editions were wanted."

XV. CARLYLE TO HIS MOTHER, SCOTSBRIG.

CHELSEA, Saturday [*February*, 1841].

MY DEAR GOOD MOTHER, — Take *half* a
word from me to-day since I have no time for
more. I had forgotten that it was Saturday
till after breakfast I learnt it, and ever since
there has been business on business!

We received your good little letter one
evening and sent it on to John. Thanks to
you for it. I had a letter too from Grahame
about his Miscellanies, for which he seems
amazingly thankful, poor fellow. We will
not tell him about the Ecclefechan Library —
let well be!

John also sends word of himself — all right
enough, the " probability " that he will be
here again before long.

Jane and I are well, rejoicing in the improved weather, not the *best* of weather yet, but immensely better than it was. Some days have been sunny and bright, a pleasant prophecy of spring.

I have *bargained* with Fraser for my lectures. They are now at press, that kept me so very busy. He would give me only £75, the dog, but then he undertakes a new edition of Sartor, too, (the former being sold) and gives me another £75 for that too. It is not so bad, £150 of ready money — at least money without risk. I did not calculate on getting anything at *present* for Teufelsdroeckh. You see we are rather rising than falling, " mall in shaft," at any rate. That is always a great point. Poor Teufelsdroeckh, it seems very curious money should lie even in him. They trampled him into the gutters at his first appearance, but he rises up again, — finds money bid for him.

On the whole I expect not to be obliged to lecture this year, which will be an immense relief to me: I shall not be broken in pieces, I shall have strength for perhaps some better things than lecturing.

You spoke of going to Dumfries: I am always afraid of your getting hurt on those expeditions, but I suppose you will not be able to rest without going. I wish Jean and you both were through it.

By the bye, did I ever sufficiently tell Isabella that her butter continues excellent, none better. I owe Jamie a letter too. Alick ought to have been apprised how good his bacon was — *was*, for alas, I myself eat the most part of it and it is done : some weeks ago his tobacco ran out ; I never told this either — I forgot everything !

Well, dear Mother, this is all I can say in my hurry. I will write again soon, but with two Books at the printer's with &c., &c., what can a poor man do ? Be good bairns, one and all of you.

Your ever affectionate
T. CARLYLE.

When the proofs of Hero-Worship were finished, visits to Richard Monckton Milnes (afterward Lord Houghton), and to the James Marshalls at Headingly, gave Carlyle what seem to have been his first glimpses of life in great country houses. On the 17th of April, 1841, he communicated his impressions to his wife : " I never lived before in such an element of ' much ado about *almost* Nothing ; ' life occupied altogether in getting itself lived ; . . . and such champagning, claretting, and witty conversationing. *Ach Gott!* I would sooner be a ditcher than spend *all* my days so. However, we got rather tolerably through it for these ten days." Visits to his mother, Miss Martineau, the Speddings, and a month in lodgings at Newby — where he probably did not think of Redgauntlet — disposed of most of the remaining holiday, and brought Carlyle back to Cheyne Row in September. The book would not yet begin itself. " Ought I to write now of Oliver Cromwell? *Gott weiss;* I cannot yet see clearly." Toward the close of this year, Carlyle was asked to let himself be nominated to the new History Chair in Edinburgh University. He declined, with noble thanks.

" Our brother," whom Carlyle writes of to Mrs. Hanning, was their half-brother, already referred to, who had emigrated to Canada in 1837, and died there in 1872.

XVI. CARLYLE TO MRS. HANNING, DUMFRIES.

CHELSEA, 24 *Nov'r*, 1841.

DEAR JENNY, — Here is the American letter you spoke of. It arrived yesterday, and to-day, after showing it to John, I send it to you. I do not exactly know what part of Canada it is dated from, but the place lies some hundreds of miles northwest of where your husband is likely to be. Our brother seems to be going on in a very prosperous way there.

On Sunday last the Doctor showed me a letter he had written for you. It appeared to be full of rational advice, in all of which I agree. You must pluck up a spirit, my good little Jenny, and see clearly how many things you yourself, independent of all other persons, can still do. *You*, then, can either act like a wise, courageous person or like a fool, between which two ways of it there lies still all the difference in the world for you. . . . I assert, and believe always, that no person whatever can be ruined except *by his own consent, by his own act*, in this world. Your little bairn will get to walk, then you will have more time to sit to some kind of employment. This will be your first consolation.

I know not whether our Mother is still with you, but suppose yes. I wrote to her a very hurried scrawl last week. Pray take good care of her from the damp and cold. I

will write to her again before long. By
Alick's letter of yesterday I learn that the
Doctor's Book for her is safely come to Ecclefechan. You can tell her farther that I
have now settled finally about her *Luther*
and it is *hers*. The cost was only some 26
shillings instead of 28.

Jane has again over-hauled the drawers
which you had such work with; the best
plan was found to be to clip the leg off altogether and put in four new inches *above the
knee!* Good be with you, dear Jenny, with
you, and them all.

It is evident from one letter and another
that, after the removal to Dumfries and Mr.
Hanning's departure for Canada, Mrs. Hanning spent more time at the Gill than in
Dumfries. "Poor Helen" was Helen Mitch-
ell from Kirkcaldy, an entertaining as well
as a faithful servant. She came to Cheyne
Row toward the end of 1837, was reclaimed
from drink by Mrs. Carlyle, but fell hope-
lessly into it again after eleven years of service. "Her end was sad, and like a thing
of fate."

XVII. CARLYLE TO HIS MOTHER, SCOTSBRIG.

CHELSEA, *8th January*, 1842.

MY DEAR MOTHER, — You have been wandering so about of late times, and there has been such confused trouble going on, that I have not got you regularly written to. It seems to me a long while since we had any right communication together. To-day I will scribble you a word before going out. Alick says you are for moving over to Gill again to bear Jenny company till the day lengthens. If you be already gone they will send this after you.

The great trouble there has been at Scotsbrig must have been distressing to every person there, from the poor father and mother downwards. You, in particular, could not escape. The weather also is sorely inclement and not wholesome for those that cannot take violent exercise; yet Alick assures me you are " as well as usual." Nay, he adds that you mean soon to write to me. I pray you take care, dear Mother, in your shifting to the Gill and during your stay there in the stranger house; it is bitter weather and looks as if it would continue long frosty. Tell me especially how you are, what clothes you

wear, whether you get good fires. A warm
bottle is indispensable in the bed at night.
You have books to read, daily little bits of
work to do; you must crouch quiet till the
sun comes out again.

A considerable noise has been going on
about that little Review-Article of mine which
I sent you. The last page *of the Divine
Right of Squires* has been circulating widely
through the Newspapers with various com-
mentary and so forth. This I by no means
grudge: as the thing is true, it may circulate
as widely as it likes. It can do nothing but
good (whether pleasant or painful *good*) being *true*, — let it circulate where it will. If
a word of mine can help to relieve the world
from an insupportable oppression, surely it
shall be very welcome to do so! The man
has paid me for this "article" (£24) but I
think I shall not soon trouble the world again
with reviewing. I mean something *else* than
that if I could get at it. On the whole, what
with Edinburgh Professorships, what with
Covenanter Articles, we have had rather a
noisy time of it in the newspapers for a while
back. It is not unpleasant, but except for
aiding the sale of one's books, perhaps it is
apt to be unprofitable. Fame? Reputation?

&c, as old Tom White said of the whisky, " *Keep* your whisky to yoursel'! deevil o' ever I 'se better than when there 's no a drop on 't i' my wame ? " which is a literal *truth,* — both as to fame and whisky.

My new book, I may tell you now, is to be something about that same *Civil War in England* which Baillie was in the midst of ; I think mainly or almost exclusively about *Oliver Cromwell.* I am struggling sore to get some hold of it, but the business will be dreadfully difficult, far worse than any *French Revolution,* if I am to do it *right :* — and if I do not do it *right* what is the use of doing it at all ? For some time I tried actual writing at it lately, but found it was too *soon* yet. I must wrestle and tumble about with it, indeed at bottom I do not know yet whether *ever* I shall be able to make a Book out of it ! All that I can do is to *try,* till I ascertain either Yes or No. For the rest I am grown too old and cunning now to plunge right on and attempt conquering the thing by sheer *force.* I lie back, *canny, canny,* and whenever I find my sleep beginning to suffer, I lay down the tools for a while. By Heaven's great blessing I am not now urged on by direct need of money. We have arranged ourselves here in what to London people is an inconceivable state of *thrift*, and in our small way are not now tormented with any fear of want whatever, for the present. To myself my poverty is really quite a suitable, almost comfortable, arrangement. I often think what should I do if I *were* wealthy! I am perhaps among the freest men in the British Empire at this moment. No King or Pontiff has any power over me, gets any revenue from me, except what he may *deserve* at my hands. There is nothing but my Maker whom I call Master under this sky. What would I be at? George Fox was hardly freer in his *suit of leather* than I here: if to be sure not carrying it quite so far as the *leather*. Jane, too, is quite of my way of thinking in this respect. Truly we have been mercifully dealt with, and much that looked like evil has turned to be good. One thing I must tell you as a small adventure which befell, the day before yesterday. On going out for walking along one of these streets an elderly, innocent, intelligent-looking gentleman accosted me with " Apologies for introducing himself to Mr. Carlyle whose works &c, &c. He was *the Parish clergyman*," rector of the Parish of St. Luke's,

Chelsea! I replied of course with all civility to the worthy man (though shocked to admit that after seven years of parishionership I did not know the face of him). We walked together as far as our roads would coincide, then parted with low bows. I mean to ask about the man (whose *name* I do not even know yet!) and, if the accounts be good, to invite a nearer approximation.

Jack will be with us to-morrow evening, we expect; oftenest we see him only that once in the course of a week. He is healthy, cheery and as full of talk and activity as I ever saw him. His Patient and he walk daily, or drive, or ride several hours, which is a good encourager of health. He seems likelier than ever to stay a good while in this present situation, to realize a good purse perhaps, — and then retire as a half-pay. Jane sticks close in the house ever since the frost began, for near a week now; she is in very tolerable health. Poor Helen, our servant, heard the other night of the death of a poor sick (asthmatic) sister at Edinburgh, which grieved her to the ground for a while and still greatly afflicts her; we are sorry for the poor creature.

Alick's long letter, you can tell him, shall

be answered by and by. I had also a letter from Jean not many days ago. I have extremely little time for writing letters. You must all be patient with me. Commend me to poor Isabella, whose affliction we deeply sympathize with.   Yours affectionately.

On February 26th Mrs. Welsh died at Templand, in Nithsdale, where she had lived since her daughter's marriage. Carlyle had now to pass two months and more at Templand in the settlement of affairs. By the death of her mother Mrs. Carlyle regained possession of Craigenputtock, the rent of which, £200 a year, she had settled on Mrs. Welsh for her life. "Thus, from this date onward," notes Carlyle in the Reminiscences, "we were a little richer, easier in circumstances; and the *pinch* of Poverty, which had been relaxing latterly, changed itself into a gentle *pressure*, or into a *limit* and little more. We did not change our habits in any point, but the grim collar round my neck was sensibly slackened. Slackened, not removed at all, — for almost twenty years yet. . . . I do not think my literary income was above £200 a year in those decades, — in spite of my continual diligence day by day."

The " cheery little cousin " was Miss Jeannie Welsh, daughter to John Welsh of Liverpool, before mentioned, and mentioned again in the last paragraph of the following letter.

XVIII. CARLYLE TO HIS MOTHER, SCOTSBRIG.

CHELSEA, Friday, *4th June*, 1842.

MY DEAR MOTHER, — A letter from Jenny came in the beginning of the week; then last night another from her for Jack, which seemed to have been written at the same time, which also I opened as it passed, — forwarding them both thereupon to Jack. Jack's address is 3 Chester Terrace, Regent's Park. Tell Jenny to copy this, and then she will know it henceforth. You must also thank her very kindly for the word she sends me about you and about the rest. I find your eyes are still sore, and I doubt this hot weather will do them no good. Perhaps keeping out of the light as much as possible might be useful. I would also recommend to *abstain from rubbing* as much as you can. If Jack know any likely eye water, I will make him send a receipt for it. This is a very troublesome kind of thing : — but surely we ought to be thankful that it is not a worse thing too !

Jack was away in the country last week, but is come home again. He was down here on Wednesday night to tea, as fresh and hearty as ever. They are to be in London mainly, I believe, all summer. He will contrive plenty of " jaunts " &c., I suppose. It is, as formerly, an idle trade, but a very well paid one. It was precisely on that Wednesday that the Queen had been shot at. These are bad times for Kings and Queens. This young blackguard, it seems, is *not* mad at all; was in great want, and so forth; it is said they will hang him. Such facts indicate that even among the lowest classes of the people, Queenship and Kingship are fast growing out of date.

My poor wife is still very disconsolate, silent, pale, broken-down, and very weak. I urge her out as much as possible; her cheery little cousin, too, does what she can. Alas, it is a very sore affliction; we have but one mother to lose. I speak to her seriously sometimes, but speaking cannot heal grief; only Time and Heaven's mercy can.

As for me, I sleep tolerably well, and also have now begun to work a little, which is still better! I shall have a terrible heap of reading, of meditating, sorting, struggling of

every kind. But why should I not do it, if
it be a good work? I feel as if there did
lie something in it. I will grudge no toil
to bring it out. I go often all day to the
Museum Library and search innumerable old
pamphlets, &c. It is a nasty place, five miles
off, and full of heat and bad air, but it contains great quantities of information. I refuse all *dinners* whatsoever, or very nearly
all. I say, " Well, if you do take offence at
me, how can I help it? In the whole world
there is only one true blessing for me, — that
of working an honest work. If you would
give me the Bank of England, and all set to
worship me with bended knees, — alas, *that*
would do nothing for me at all. It is not
you that can help me or hinder me; it is I,
even I." Pray that I persist in this good
course.

Poor Isabella does not seem to profit by
the warm weather. I would recommend the
shower bath to her. I take it daily here.
Tell Jenny that there is no hurry about the
shirts. She can go on with all leisure. Did
Jamie ever learn from me that in the drawer
of *their* washstand, if he will pull it out,
there lies for him a little piece of new stuff
for rubbing on his razor strop? I always

forgot to mention it. Our weather here is excellent, threatening to be too hot by and by, which, however, I shall not grudge so much this year. Broiling weather to me will be the basis of a plenteous year for all. There is much need of it !

But I must end, dear Mother. I write hardly *any* letters except to you, so you will accept this as the best I can do at present. The subscription for Burns's sister is doing well, in Liverpool at least (under John Welsh). My affection to Alick and all of them. You will get this when you go to the Preaching.

My blessings on you, dear Mother, and all love.

Your son,

Tom.

XIX. CARLYLE TO HIS MOTHER, SCOTSBRIG.

Chelsea, Monday Morning,
4th July, 1842.

My dear Mother, — Before setting to my work, let me expend a penny and a scrap of paper on you, merely to say that we are well, and to send a bit of ugly and curious public news that you cannot yet have heard of. On Saturday night it was publicly made

known that Francis, the man who last shot at
the Queen, was not to be hanged, but to be
sent to Botany Bay, or some such punish-
ment. Well, yesterday about noon, as the
Queen went to St. James' Chapel, a third
individual presented his pistol at the Majesty
of England, but was struck down and seized
before he could fire it; he and another who
seemed to be in concert with him are both
laid up. There is no doubt of the fact.
The two are both "young" men; we have
yet heard nothing more of them than that.
The person who struck down the pistol (and
with it the man, so vehement was he) is said
to be a gentleman's flunkey; but I do not
know that for certain and have seen no newspaper yet. . . . Are not these strange times?
The people are sick of their misgovernment,
and the blackguards among them shoot at the
poor Queen : as a man that wanted the steeple
pulled down might at least fling a stone at
the gilt weathercock. The poor little Queen
has a horrid business of it, — cannot take a
drive in HER *clatch* without risk of being
shot! *Our* clatch is much safer. All men
are becoming alarmed at the state of the
country, — as I think they well may.

Jane and her cousin have this morning

been got off to Windsor by the Sterlings. The jaunt in the open air will do the poor Wifie good.

John is very well. I parted with him last night near his own house rather after 10 o'clock.

Adieu, dear Mother. Here is a foolish Yankee letter of adoration to me. Burn it!

Your affectionate,

T. CARLYLE.

The picture of Sartor measuring himself for shirts to be made at long range, as it were, is memorable even in the annals of Cheyne Row.

XX. CARLYLE TO MRS. HANNING, THE GILL.

CHELSEA, 21 *July*, 1842.

MY DEAR JENNY, — I am glad to hear of your well being, and that you have got done with the shirts, which is a sign of your industry. They will be well off your hands, and I have no doubt will be found very suitable when they arrive here. In the meanwhile I do not want them sent off yet till there are some more things to go with them. I am in no want of them yet, and shall not, I think, be so till it will be about time for the meal

to be sent from Scotsbrig. At all events,
you may look to that (for the present) as the
way of sending them, and therefore keep
them beside you till some chance of deliver-
ing them safe to my Mother or another Scotsbrig party turn up. There is no haste about
them ; the meal *cannot* be ready, I suppose,
till the end of September, if then.

In the meanwhile I want you to make
me some flannel things, too, — three flannel
shirts especially : you can get the flannel
from Alick, if he have any that he can well
recommend. You can readily have them
made before the other shirts go off : I have
taken the measure to-day, and now send you
the dimensions, together with a measuring
strap which I bought some weeks ago (at one
penny) for the purpose ! *You are to be careful to scour the flannel first*, after which
process the dimensions are these. *Width*
(when the shirt is laid on its back) $22\frac{1}{2}$
inches, *extent from wrist button to wrist
button* 61 inches,[1] *length* in the back 35
inches, *length* in the front $25\frac{1}{2}$ inches. Do
you understand all that ? I dare say you
will make it out, and this measuring band
will enable you to be exact enough. Only

---

[1] So that each sleeve is $19\frac{1}{4}$ inches long.

you must observe that at the beginning of it.
. . . Hoity-Toity ! I find that it is I myself
that have made a mistake there, and that you
have only to measure fair with the line and
all will be right; the dimensions as above,
$22\frac{1}{2}$, 61, 35, $25\frac{1}{2}$.

If you could make me two pairs of flannel
drawers, I should like very well too, but
that I am afraid will be too hard for you.
This is all the express work I have for you
at present. Neither is there any news of
much moment that I could send you. Jane
continues still weak, but seems to gather
strength, too. I keep very quiet and very
busy, and stand the summer fully better than
is usual with me here. John still continues
in town, and does not speak of going yet.
We meet every Sunday here at Dinner.

Our good Mother, you perhaps know, has
got over to Jean for some sea bathing about
Arbigland. We hope they are all well about
Gill, and that a good crop is on its feet for
them. Give our kind regards and continual
good wishes both to Mary and Jamie, and accept them for yourself. Next time you write
you had better tell me how your money
stands out ; and if at any time, my dear little
Sister, I can help you in anything, be sure

do not neglect to write *then*.   Our love and
best wishes to you, dear Jenny.

Your affectionate brother,

T. CARLYLE.

In May, on his way back from Templand, Carlyle had stopped to visit Dr. Arnold
at Rugby, and in August he went to Bel-
gium with Mr. Stephen Spring Rice and
his younger brother.   Of this trip Carlyle
wrote an extraordinarily vivid account under
title of The Shortest Tour on Record.   The
picture of the poor lace-maker and her habitation, at Ghent, makes one think, by a
queer, austere contrary, of an earlier traveler
and his adventures.

In August, also, Mrs. Carlyle had gone to
the Bullers', in Suffolk.   Twenty capital
pages of Letters and Memorials make her
visit live again.

XXI.   CARLYLE TO HIS MOTHER, SCOTSBRIG.

CAMBRIDGE, *7th Sep.*, 1842.

MY DEAR MOTHER, — I am sitting here in
the " Hoop Inn " of Cambridge, in a spacious apartment, blazing with gaslight and
nearly solitary.   It strikes me I may as well
employ the hour before bedtime in writing a

word for my good Mother, — to explain to her how I am, and above all what in the world I am doing here! There is a magnificent thunderstorm just going on, or rather beginning to pass off in copious floods of rain, and there is no other sound audible in this room; one single fellow-traveller lies reading the Times Newspaper on the sofa opposite, and the rain quenches even the sound of his breath.

Well, dear Mother, you heard that Jane was gone into Suffolk to Mrs. Buller's, and perhaps you understand or guess that she continues still there; nay, perhaps Jack may have informed you that on Thursday last (a week ago all but a day) I, after long higgling, set out to bring her home. Home, however, she was not to go quite so fast. Mrs. Buller, rather lively up in that region, wanted her to stay a little longer, wanted me also, I suppose, to go flaunting about, calling on Lady this and Sir Henry that, and *lionizing* and amusing myself as I best might in her neighbourhood. She is very kind indeed, — more hospitable and good than I have almost ever seen her to anybody. The place Troston is a quiet, sleek, green place, so intersected with green, wide lanes (loanings)

all overgrown with trees that you can hardly
find your way in it, — like walking in some
coal-mine in paths underground ; it or any
green country whatever, as you know, is
likely to be welcome to me. One day I
walked off to a place called Thetford in
Norfolk, about 8 miles from us. It was the
morrow after my arrival, and I did not know
the nature of the lanes then. I lost my way
both going and coming, and made the distance 12 or 13 each way, but got home in
time to dinner, and was all the better for my
walk. Afterwards I never ventured out of
sight of Troston Church-tower without first
drawing for myself a little map of my route
from a big map that hangs in the lobby.
With my little map in my waistcoat pocket
I feared nothing, and indeed in three days
knew all the outs and ins of the country ; —
for Mrs. Buller in that interval had contrived
to borrow me a farmer's horse to go about
on. Was not that a friendly office to a man
like me ?

But to hasten to the point ! Mrs. Buller's,
I knew beforehand, was but some 30 miles to
the east of Cromwell's country ; his birthplace, the farm he had first, and the farm he
had second, all lie adjoining on the West-

ward, either in the next County, which is this (Cambridgeshire), or in Huntingdonshire, the one Westward of this. Accordingly, having talked a long enough time about jaunts and pilgrimages, — about it and about it, — I decided at last (the women threatening to laugh at me if I did not go) on actually setting off, and accordingly here I am, with my face already homewards, the main part of my little errand successfully accomplished; and a " riding tour " through the country parts of England, which I have been talking of these dozen years or more, has actually taken effect on the small scale, — a very *small* scale indeed. I have ridden but two days, and on the morrow evening I shall be at Troston again, or near it. My conveyance being the farmer's horse above mentioned, my fatigue has been great ; — for it is the roughest and dourest beast nearly that I ever rode, and to-day in the morning, to mend matters, it took to the trick they call " scouring," — in a sullen, windless ninny niawing. — Many a time I thought of Alick and Jamie in these Cambridge Fens, and wished one or both of them had been near me. But I let the creature take time (for it *would* have it), and it gradually recruited again, though not brilliant at

the best; and indeed I shall be very willing
to wish it good-bye to-morrow evening, were
I at Troston again. Poor brute, *it* cannot
help being supple and riding as with stilky-
clogs at its feet! It has eaten four and a
half feeds of corn to-day, or I think it would
altogether have failed.

But at any rate I have *seen* the Cromwell
country, got an image of it in my mind for
all time henceforth. I was last night at Ely,
the Bishop's City of this district. I walked
in and about the Cathedral for two good
hours. Thought vividly of Cromwell step-
ping up these floors, with his sword by his
side, bidding the Priest (who would not obey
his *first* order, but continued reading his lit-
urgies), "Cease your fooling and come out,
Sir." — One can fancy with what a *gollie* in
the voice of him. I found the very house
he had lived in. I sat and smoked a pipe
about nine o'clock under the stars on the
very "Horseblock" (*harping-on stone*) which
Oliver had often mounted from, two hundred
years ago. It was all full of interest, and
though I could get but very little sleep at
night, I did not grudge that price. To-day
I rode still farther Westward to a place called
St. Ives, where Oliver first took to farming.

The house they showed as his I did not believe in, but the fields that he tilled and reaped are veritably there. I sat down under the shade of one of his hedges and kindled a cigar, not without reflections! I have also seen his native town Huntingdon, with many other things to-day, and am here now on my way homeward, as I said, and will not trouble my dear good Mother with one other word of babblement on the subject at present. No country *in itself* can well be uglier; it is all a drained immensity of fen (or soft peat moss), and bears a considerable resemblance to the trench at Dumfries, — if that were some 30 or 40 miles square, with Parish churches innumerable, all built on dry knolls of chalky earth that rise up like islands. You can tell Jamie that it bears *heary* crops! oats, beans, wheat, which they are just concluding the leading in of at present; the rest of the country being done a week or two ago.

Dear Mother, was there ever such a clatter of a letter written? And not one word of news, not one word even of the many hundred I could use in inquiring! We return to Chelsea, I expect, about Monday *first*. Saturday was to be proposed, but will not stand

I believe. Jack is already gone, on Saturday last, to Cheltenham, and then for North Wales. Right glad am I for him and for you that he is to come into Annandale for a little while. Poor fellow, it is long since he has been there, and he too has his own feelings and straits which he does not speak about often. My dear Mother, I will bid you all good-night. I send you my heart's best blessing o'er all the hills and rivers that lie between us to-night. The thunder is gone, and the rain. I will send you a little word when we get to Chelsea; perhaps there is something from yourself for me already forwarded to Troston. I doubt it. Good-night, my dear true Mother.

Ever your affect^e
T. CARLYLE.

I know not whether Alick has now any communication with the Whitehaven Tobacconist? A quarter of a stone might be ventured upon along with the Harvest meal, or by the Doctor or some other conveyance. It keeps in the winter; it could not be *worse* than my London tobacco all this year. Tell Alick about it; he rejoices always to help me whenever he can.

Carlyle's pilgrimage to Huntingdon, St. Ives, and thereabouts, is not to be confounded with his former Cromwell journey — to Naseby — undertaken a few months before, with Dr. Arnold. Froude's account of Carlyle's investigation of the battlefield was (necessarily) so incomplete that I venture to quote here two highly interesting letters from a long afterward published book, — Letters of Edward Fitzgerald. Says Fitzgerald, in a memorandum on the subject : —

" As I happened to know the Field well, — the greater part of it then belonging to my Family, — I knew that Carlyle and Arnold had been mistaken — misled in part by an Obelisk which my Father had set up as on the highest Ground of the Field, but which they mistook for the centre-ground of the Battle. This I told Carlyle, who was very reluctant to believe that he and Arnold could have been deceived — that he could accept no hearsay Tradition or Theory against the Evidence of his own Eyes, etc. However, as I was just then going down to Naseby, I might enquire further into the matter.

" On arriving at Naseby, I had spade and mattock taken to a hill near half a mile across from the 'Blockhead Obelisk,' and pitted with several hollows, overgrown with rank Vegetation, which Tradition had always pointed to as the Graves of the Slain. One of these I had opened; and there, sure enough, were the remains of skeletons closely packed together — chiefly teeth — but some remains of Shin-bone, and marks of Skull in the Clay. Some of these, together with some sketches of the Place, I sent to Carlyle."

Fitzgerald, in a letter which has apparently not been preserved, sent the results of this first investigation to Carlyle. He wrote also from Naseby the following letter to Bernard Barton : —

[NASEBY], *Septr.* **22**, /42.

MY DEAR BARTON, — The pictures are left all ready packed up in Portland Place, and shall come down with me, whenever that desirable event takes place. In the meanwhile here I am as before; but having received a long and interesting letter from Carlyle asking information about this Battle field, I have trotted about rather more to ascertain names of places, positions, etc. After all, he will make a mad book. I have just seen some of the bones of a dragoon and his horse who were found foundered in a morass in the field — poor dragoon, much dismembered by time: his less worthy members, having been left in the owner's summer-house for the last twenty years, have disappeared one by one, but his skull is kept safe in the hall : not a bad skull neither ; and in it some teeth yet holding, and a bit of the iron heel of his boot, put into the skull by way of convenience. This is what Sir Thomas Browne calls "making a man act his Antipodes."[1] I have got a fellow to dig at one of the great general graves in the field ; and he tells me to-night that he has come to bones ; to-morrow I will select a neat specimen or two. In the meantime let the full harvest moon wonder at them as they lie turned up after lying hid 2400 revolutions of hers. Think of that warm 14th of June when the Battle was fought, and they fell pell-mell : and then the country people came and buried them so shallow that the stench was terrible, and the putrid matter oozed over the ground for several yards ; so that the cattle were observed to eat those places very close for some years after. Every one

[1] Referring to a passage in the Garden of Cyrus, near the end : " To keep our eyes open longer, were but to act our antipodes. The huntsmen are up in America, and they are already past their first sleep in Persia."

to his taste, as one might well say to any woman who kissed the cow that pastured there.

Friday, 23rd. We have dug at a place, as I said, and made such a trench as would hold a dozen fellows, whose remains positively make up the mould. The bones nearly all rotted away, except the teeth, which are quite good. At the bottom lay the form of a perfect skeleton : most of the bones gone, but the pressure distinct in the clay ; the thigh and leg bones yet extant ; the skull a little pushed forward, as if there were scanty room. We also tried some other reputed graves, but found nothing ; indeed, it is not easy to distinguish what are graves from old marlpits, etc. I don't care for all this bone-rummaging myself ; but the identification of the graves identifies also where the greatest heat of the battle was. Do you wish for a tooth ?

As I began this antiquarian account in a letter to you, so I have finished it, that you may mention it to my Papa, who perhaps will be amused at it. Two farmers insisted on going out exploring with me all day : one a very solid fellow, who talks like the justices in Shakespeare, but who certainly was inspired in finding out this grave ; the other a

Scotchman, full of intelligence, who proposed
the flesh-soil for manure for turnips. The
old Vicar, whose age reaches halfway back
to the day of the Battle, stood tottering over
the verge of the trench. Carlyle has shewn
great sagacity in guessing at the localities
from the vague descriptions of contempora-
ries; and his short *pasticcio* of the battle is
the best I have seen. But he will spoil all
by making a demigod of Cromwell, who certainly was so far from wise that he brought
about the very thing he fought to prevent, —
the restoration of an unrestricted monarchy.

The substance of this letter was of course
communicated by Fitzgerald to Carlyle, who
promptly and gratefully replied.

CHELSEA, Saturday, 25 [24] *Septr.* 1842.

MY DEAR SIR, — You will do me and the
Genius of History a real favour, if you persist in these examinations and excavations to
the utmost length possible for you! It is
long since I read a letter so interesting as
yours of yesterday. Clearly enough you are
upon the very battle-ground ; — and I, it is
also clear, have only looked up towards it
from the slope of Mill Hill. Were not the

weather so wet, were not, etc., etc., so many etceteras, I could almost think of running up to join you still! But that is evidently *un*-feasible at present.

The opening of that burial-heap blazes strangely in my thoughts : these are the very jawbones that were clenched together in deadly rage, on this very ground, 197 years ago! It brings the matter home to one, with a strange veracity, — as if for the first time one saw it to be no fable and theory, but a dire fact. I will beg for a tooth and a bullet ; authenticated by your own eyes and word of honour! Our Scotch friend, too, making turnip manure of it, — he is part of the Picture. I understand almost all the Netherlands battlefields have already given up their bones to British husbandry ; why not the old English next ? Honour to thrift. If of 5000 wasted men you can make a few usable turnips, why, do it !

The more sketches and details you can contrive to send me, the better. I want to know, for one thing, whether there is any *house* on Cloisterwell ; what house that was that I saw from the slope of Naseby height (Mill-hill, I suppose), and fancied to be Dust Hill Farm ? It must lie about North by

West from Naseby Church, perhaps near a mile off. You say, one cannot see Dust Hill at all, much less any farm house of Dust Hill, from that Naseby Height?

But why does the Obelisk stand there? It might as well stand at Charing Cross; the blockhead that it is! I again wish I had wings; alas, I wish many things; that the gods would but annihilate Time and Space, which would include all things!

In great haste, Yours most truly,

T. CARLYLE.

Both Carlyle's letter to Fitzgerald and that to his mother from Cambridge are notable illustrations of the insatiable hunger of the eye which went far to make him the great writer he was. The print of those teeth on his mind is shown in Cromwell, where we read: "A friend of mine has in his cabinet two ancient grinder-teeth, dug lately from that ground, — and waits for an opportunity to rebury them there. Sound, effectual grinders, one of them very large; which ate their breakfast on the fourteenth morning of June, two hundred years ago, and, except to be clenched once in grim battle, had never work to do more in this world!"

The old mother was not ungrateful for her son's mindfulness. Nothing in their relations is more touching than the brevity and stiffness of her letters, with every now and then some burst of natural affection which even the artificial medium cannot check. Margaret Carlyle had learned to write in adult life for the sake of replying to her son's letters, but the pen never became an obedient instrument in her hand. She could always have sympathized with Joe Gargery.

XXII.   TO CARLYLE FROM HIS MOTHER.

SCOTSBRIG, *Sept.* 13, 1812.

MY DEAR SON, — It is a long time since you had a word from me, though I have had many kind letters from you, for which if I am not thankful enough, I am glad. I am full as well as I was when you saw me last. I am reading the poem on " Luther " and I am much pleased with it. I wish the author Godspeed. It is a good subject and well handled, is my opinion of it. I had a letter from John yesterday, he thinks he will see us in the Course of a month or so. We will be glad to see him again if it please God. We have excellent weather here. I do not remember such a summer and harvest. Jamie had a good crop and very near all in and well got up. Isabel is still poorly. She is rather better than she was at one time. How are you after your wanderings? Write as soon as you can and tell us all your news.

Ever your affectionate Mother,

M. A. C.

XXIII. TO MRS. HANNING, AT THE GILL, FROM HER MOTHER.

SCOTSBRIG, Monday [1810-1851].

MY DEAR JENNY, — I have been longing for you to come here for a long time. I want to send two hams on to London. Could you get a box which would hold the shirts and both could be sent at the same time. If you have not sent them any, bring them over as soon as you can, and come soon. At any rate bring the winter things that Jean sent. We are all in our frail way of health. Give my kindest love to young and old.

Ever your old mother,

M. A. C.

In the letter subjoined, Carlyle gives his mother the conclusion of his visit to the Bullers, of which he had written so fully.

" The good Mrs. Strachey," sister to Mrs. Buller, was the pious widow of a rich examiner in the India House.   Mr. Strachey, eighteen years before, had accompanied Carlyle to Paris.   " Min " must have been a household name for Miss Jeannie Welsh.

XXIV.   CARLYLE TO HIS MOTHER, SCOTSBRIG.

CHELSEA, 19th Sept. 1842.

MY DEAR MOTHER, — Will you take the smallest of notes from me merely to perform the essential function of a note, — ask you how you are and say that I am well.

I wrote you ten days ago a long letter dated Cambridge from my Inn in that Town. This I hope you received duly.   It would let you into my ways in those weeks.   Next day I got well enough back to Troston, rain attending me for the last two hours.   I was terribly wearied of my great flat-soled monster of a horse, but much gratified with my pilgrimage and all rejoiced very handsomely at my return.   Charles had come in the interim.   They would not let us away on Monday as we proposed.   It was settled at last that Thursday should be the day.   Charles came up with us to Town.   We had a very pleasant kind of journey and got safe home to dinner here. So ends the Troston journey and I think all travelling for this season. The good Mrs. Strachey, who is now in Italy, wrote to offer us her house and servants for two months at Clifton, a beautiful Village near Bristol, 100 miles to the west of us, but we have refused. Rolling stone gathers little bog. I must resolutely get some work done now.

Jane seems really better for her country excursion. I observed to-day that she eats a whole slice of bread to breakfast again. Little Min W. is still here. I think she likes much better to be here than at home, in the midst of luxury but also of Liverpool stupidity. She is a fine cheery little lass, very pretty too, and would make a good wife for somebody.

The Duke of Buccleuch has now actually *paid* me the £100 — at least sent a draft payable in 10 days hence. I sent my thanks and the business is all over — a right agreeable result. You may tell Jamie that the Templand Grates too are paid, payable at the same time; that we *saved* the Grates that day, and our broiling journey was not in vain, therefore.

I hope they have now all got a sight of

your picture and that I shall get it soon. It
will be needless to wait for Jack, he, as I reflect, can do nothing towards carrying it.
Poor fellow — you will see him again. Here
is his last letter, though it can have no news
for you. How goes Jamie's harvest? The
weather has been *brittle* ever since that thunderstorm. How go you yourself, my dear
good Mother? Somebody ought to write to
me now. I do not hear anything even from
Jean. Could Jenny make me two pairs of
flannel drawers along with the shirts? I
fear not. Adieu, dear Mother, my love to
one and all.

T. CARLYLE.

XXV. CARLYLE TO MRS. HANNING, THE GILL.

CHELSEA, 2d *Nov.* 1842.

MY DEAR JENNY, — Yesterday I meant to
have written to you, in order to be ready for
Thursday at Annan, such had been my firm
purpose, but something came in the way, and
I altogether forgot till this morning. Lest I
make a similar mistake for Saturday too, I
will take time by the forelock and write even
now. The barrel of meal, and the box of
garments arrived all safe, on Saturday night
last.

And I have to apprize you, as the expert needlewoman of the whole, that *all fits* with perfect correctness. I have had a pair of drawers on, and a flannel shirt, I have one of the cambric shirts on me at present: everything is as right as if it had been made under my own eye. The flannel of the shirts is excellent, they are made to the very measure. The drawers also are the *best fit* of the article I have had for several years back; two of the pairs, I observe, are of the fine flannel the shirts are of. Perhaps it will prove *too cool* for the depth of winter — perhaps not, but either way I have plenty of warmer, for that season. One of the pairs is of right shaggy flannel. My good Mother sent a fine wool plaid too and a dozen pair of socks, few mortals are better off for woolen this winter! — As to the muslin shirts Jane says they are excellently sewed, — She is the judge, I find them to lie *flat* on the breast too, which the old would never do.

In short, it is all perfectly right; and you will be very glad, I doubt not, that you have got it well off your hands. If in the course of the winter, you fall *out of work*, and want a canny job for yourself, it will be acceptable enough to me that you set Jean upon getting you some more stuff, and make me half a dozen more of the like shirts ! But this you need not, unless in the aforesaid case. I believe the stock I have will serve me some couple of years or more. But they eat no bread. — If you ever do think of this, you can let me know before starting ; I may perhaps have some remarks to make.

You will be nestling all under cover now at Gill, when the short days and the frosts are come. I hope you have a right stock of fuel in your end of the house ; and that your little carpet is now complete. I long to question the Dr. about you when he comes back hither. He is at a place they call Malvern some 120 miles west of this.

How are Mary and Jamie ? very busy, and well, I hope. Mary never writes. I sent James a tobacco-box ! — Poor Allan Cunningham the Poet is dead very suddenly ; a sad event for several of us ! —

Adieu, Dear little sister.

Ever your affect.
T. Carlyle.

Much as Carlyle had been thinking about Cromwell, another book was to come first, — a book for which his very trip to Cromwell's

Chelsea, 4 May, 1843 –

Dear Jenny,

I had your letter the other day, and was glad to hear you had got back to Gill, when Mary as we understand has need of you at present then. These are terribly hard times for farmers; but they must not be disheartened: it is not likely the times will continue so bad; and if they do, some new arrangement will have to be fallen upon, — not by them alone but by the whole farming world. Tell Mary to take care and not overwork herself in her present state. Do you for her whatsoever you can in the way of help and support; I know you will without my telling you. — I like well to hear of your teaching the two little Bairns to read; that is a right good work, in which there will lie a bles-

-ing if in any words whatsoever. —

But the special object of this part in of a Note was to let you know that you are likely to see the Doctor again very soon. He is off this morning to Liverpool; and may perhaps be over in Annandale on Monday or Tuesday if there be steam on either of these days. He will of course look in upon the Gill not long after that; but it is who will tell you all our news much better than I can write them. He talks of staying "for a week or two", that is to say, as long as he finds it pleasant and useful for him and for all of you: he is in very good health and spirits; but full of uncertainty as to fixing himself, — which I wish much, but hardly hope, he could ever do.

We had a Box from Scotsbrig last night; all safe, and the contents excellent. I add no other word today; but a hearty salutation to one and all at Gill, Jamie, Mary, Jenny, and all the Bairns down to the youngest. Ever affe Brother T. Carlyle

country was fruitful in suggestion. At St.
Ives he had seen not only Cromwell's farm,
but also St. Ives poorhouse with its inhabitants, — " in the sun," to be sure, but neither
spinsters nor knitters, nor workers after any
fashion, for the simple reason that they had
no work to do. The Chartist riots of 1842
remained in Carlyle's mind with this symbolic
picture, and by October of the same year he
was deeply pondering the condition of " the
English nation all sitting enchanted, the poor
enchanted so that they cannot work, the rich
enchanted so that they cannot enjoy." Over
against this contemporary view Carlyle set
the life of the monks of Bury St. Edmunds,
as told by their chronicler, Jocelyn de Brake-
londe ; and the result was Past and Present,
written, apparently with less struggle than
any of the author's other books, in the first
seven weeks of 1843. Although Carlyle
went too far in this work, — as indeed he
so seldom failed to do, — Past and Present
proved the germ of more than one sadly
needed reform ; and the splendid, sonorous
passage beginning, " All true work is sacred,"
will remain, one must believe, an inalienable
possession of English literature and English
morals.

Publication followed in April, and soon afterward Carlyle wrote in his Journal: "That book always stood between me and Cromwell, and now that has fledged itself and flown off." Face to face with Oliver again, Carlyle went in the summer of 1843 to see famous battlefields of the civil war. He so planned his itinerary as to reach Dunbar on the 3d of September, — the day of the fight there, the day of Worcester fight, and the day of Cromwell's death.

This professional journey was preceded by a peaceful month at Scotsbrig, and followed by a visit to Erskine which fixes the date of the next letter.

XXVI.   CARLYLE TO HIS MOTHER. SCOTSBRIG.

[LINLATHEN, *early September*, 1843.]

YESTERDAY by appointment, the good Thomas Erskine took me up at Kirkcaldy, carried me off hither on the top of the coach, bag and baggage. The day was damp and dim, not exactly wet, yet in danger of becoming very. There had been rain in the night time (Sabbath night or early on Monday morning) but there fell no more. This day again is oppressively hot, dry yet without sun or wind — a baddish "day for a stock." But

they prophesy fair weather now — which I
shall be glad of, and the whole country will
be glad, for all is white here, in sheaves and
stooks, and little got into ricks. We got
here about 5 in the evening, a great party of
people in the house (a big *Laird's* house
with *flunkeys* &c., &c.). I was heartily tired
before I got to bed. I do not think I shall
be rightly at rest till I get on ship board,
then I *will* lie down and let all men have a
care of stirring me, — they had better let the
sleeping dog lie! The Dundee steamers are
allowed to be the best on these waters, large
swift ships and very few passengers in them
at present. I spoke for my place yesterday
and am to have the best. The kind people
here will relieve me down (it is four miles off)
and then about 4 o'clock in the afternoon —
I shall — light a pipe in peace and *think* of
you all, speaking not a word. I expect to
sleep well there too, and then on Friday, perhaps about 3 o'clock, I may be at London
Bridge and home by the most convenient
conveyance to Chelsea for dinner. This, if
all go well, this ends for the present my pil-
grimings up and down the world.

Dear Mother, I wish I had gone direct
home when I left you, for it is not pleasant

somehow to be still in Scotland and far from
you. I speak not the thoughts I send towards you, for speech will not express them.
If I arrive *home* on Friday you may perhaps
find a newspaper at Ecclefechan on Sabbath
morning, Monday much likelier. God bless
you all.

T. CARLYLE.

The passage about Jeffrey in the next letter is better than the corresponding one given
by Froude. The reader who remembers Jeffrey's complaint that Carlyle was " so dreadfully in earnest," will smile at Carlyle's coun-
ter charge that Jeffrey had " too little real
seriousness in him " to " make a nice *old*
man."

XXVII. CARLYLE TO HIS MOTHER, SCOTSBRIG.

LINLATHEN, DUNDEE,
Tuesday, 12th Sep. 1843.

MY DEAR MOTHER, — According to promise, I write you another little word to announce that I am safe so far on my way, that
I embark to-morrow and hope to be home on
Friday afternoon. I am heartily desirous of
it! This last part of my travels has been
considerably the *weariest*, for I have been all

along eager chiefly to have done with it.
Jamie knows how fain I would never have
entered upon it all. He took notice of my
reluctance at Dumfries and how welcome a
shower of rain would have been to me!
However it is near ending now; and I shall
enjoy the quiet of home all the more. One
thing, dear Mother, let me straightway tell
you; that I have *not* left one of my new
shirts, that the whole six, when I fold them
duly out, are here. I grieve that you should
have had a moment's uneasiness about that
matter, which is due only to my own blind-
ness and numbness; my hope is that you did
not take it up too earnestly, but left the
matter over " till Jenny came."

I have now got two letters from Jane, the
last of them only yesterday! All is well at
Chelsea; Jack not yet settled in any lodging,
nor in the least decided what to do, but " in
a state of torpor" as Jane says " playing
with the cat." He was dining with Lady
Clare; that was the last feat recorded of
him. I was much grieved to hear that you
had somehow missed Alick's letter: has it
never yet turned up for you? I am too ig-
norant about the business to form any conjecture how it could have come about. Mean-

while it was very lucky that there came
another letter of the same date for Jack : —
this I am in hopes will be ready for me at
London when I arrive. By the bye, might
it not be that Alick had only *meant* and fully
intended to write you a letter, and then had
suddenly found that he would not have time
by that mail? Of course the two letters, if
there had been two, would come together : it
is unaccountable how *one* of them should
drop by the way. What a blessing to us to
hear that poor Alick is safe there and ready
to begin his adventure on fair terms. Jane
says his letter is of very composed tone and
" very practical looking." She seems to like
the tone of it well. I went over to Edinburgh since I last wrote. I there saw Gor-
don, saw various other friends — with more
or less of labour and fatigue. I spent a fore-
noon with Jeffrey who is very thin and fretful I think ; being at any rate weakly, he is
much annoyed at present by a hurt on his
shin — a quite insignificant thing otherwise,
which however disables him from walking.
Poor Jeffrey! he does not make a nice *old*
man, he has too little real seriousness in him
for that. On the whole I was heartily glad
to quit Edinburgh again and get away from

it into quietude across the Frith. I wrote to Jean at Dumfries one day.

"Carlyle returned from his travels very bilious," so his wife wrote to Mrs. Aitken in October, 1843, "and continues very bilious up to this hour." He could not refuse a "certain admiration" at the state of the house, which had been painted and papered in his absence. Mrs. Carlyle, with her own hands, had put down carpets, newly covered chairs and sofas, and arranged a library according to his (expressed) mind. His satisfaction lasted only three days, for on the morning of the fourth day "the young lady next door took a fit of practising on her accursed piano-forte." There had then to be another upheaval : "down went a partition in one room, up went a new chimney in another ; " and still another library, farther from the piano, was thus contrived. Finally, the young lady, charmed by "a seductive letter" from Carlyle, agreed never to play until two in the afternoon. The dinner hour was changed to the middle of the day, because Carlyle thought it would be better for his digestion.

Although these changes, which in Mrs.

Carlyle's account seem planet-shaking, were
in the interest of Cromwell, Cromwell remained persistently unwritable. On the 4th
of December the historian wrote to Sterling :
"Confound it ! I have lost four years of
good labour in the business; and still the
more I expend on it, it is like throwing good
labour after bad." Two days later he put a
better face on it to his mother.

XXVIII. CARLYLE TO HIS MOTHER. SCOTSBRIG.

CHELSEA, Monday, *6th Dec.* 1843.

MY DEAR MOTHER, — We have a letter
from Jean this week, who reports a visit to
you and gives us a description of what you
were about. We were very glad to look in
upon you in that way. Jean describes you
as very well when they came, but since then
(though she tells us of your prohibition to
mention it at all) there has been some ill
turn of health which we long greatly to hear
of the removal of ! I study, dear Mother,
not to afflict myself with useless anxieties,
but on the whole it is much better that one
knows exactly how matters do stand, the very
fact, no better and no worse than it is. To-
day there was a little Note from James Aitken apprising us that the Books are come,

that Jenny is with him. He has evidently heard nothing farther from Scotsbrig, so we will hope things may have got into their usual course again there. But Jamie or somebody may write us a scrap of intelligence, surely? . . .

This is said to be a very unhealthy season here; for the past two months about two hundred more deaths in the week have occurred than is usual at this season, but I rather conjecture it is the result of the long continued hardship the Poor have been suffering, which now, after wearing out the constitution by hunger and distress of mind, begins to tell more visibly! Our weather is very mild, soft without any great quantity of rain and not at all disagreeable. Jane's cold is gone again and we are in our common way.

My Book goes on badly, yet I do think it goes on, in fact it must go: Bore away at it with continuous boring day and night and it will be obliged to go! I study however not to "split my gall" with it, but to "hasten slowly" as the old Romans said. When writing will not brother with me at all, I fling it entirely by and go and walk many a mile in the country. I have big thick shoes, my jacket is waterproof against slight rain, I take a stick in my hand and walk with long strides. The farther I walk, the abler I grow; in fact I am rather in better health, I think, than usual, if all things are considered. Jack and I had a long walk after Tailors for some three hours in the moonlight streets last night. To-day it is damp, but I am for a sally again. Alas, it is but a very poor morning task I have done, but we cannot help it. Adieu, dear good Mother, for our sakes take care of yourself. My love to all.

Yours affection^{ly}
T. CARLYLE.

Carlyle never liked any portrait of himself. The one mentioned in the following letter had made him look like " a flayed horse's head."

XXIX.   CARLYLE TO HIS MOTHER, SCOTSBRIG.

CHELSEA, 10th March, 1841.

MY DEAR MOTHER, — It is a shame for me if I do not write a bit of a letter to you. There is nothing else I can do for you at present. I will scribble you a few words of news on this paper, let other employments fare as they can for the present.

I sent your good little note to the Doctor. Jamie's letter for Alick came duly to hand and was duly forwarded; I also wrote a letter to Alick myself. Poor fellow, I suppose he has had a very solitary, meditative winter of it over in America, and has no doubt had a great many reflections in his head, looking back and looking forward, with perhaps sadness enough, but it will do him good, I really believe. Perhaps this winter, seemingly one of the idlest he has had, may turn out to be one of the most profitably occupied. My own hope and persuasion is that he will now do well, that he is probably about to begin a new course of activity on better terms than before, better terms both inward and outward, and that in fine, poor fellow, he may begin to see the fruit of his labor round him and go on with much more peace and prosperity than heretofore. . . . I also like the tone of his letters, which is much quieter than it used to be. He does not know, I suppose, in what direction he is to go when April arrives. I urged, as Jamie did, that a *healthy* quality of situation should outweigh all other considerations whatever, that for the

rest all places seemed to me much alike ; if
the land were cheap, it would be unfavour-
ably situated &c. I also hinted my notion
that a small piece of *good* handy soil might
be preferable to a large lot of untowardly,
outlying ground. We can only hope and
pray he may *be* guided *well.* We cannot
assist him with any real guidance. Difficul-
ties beset a man everywhere under this sun.
There if he have patience, insight, energy
and justness of mind he will daily conquer
farther, — not otherwise, either in America
or here. But, as I said, I have never lost
hope with Alick, and I have now better hope
than ever. We will commit him to the all-
wise Governor with many a prayer from the
bottom of all our hearts that it may be well
with him. To hear and know that he does
see good under the sun, fighting his way like
a true man in that new country ! — what a
comfort to you and to every one of us. My
dear Mother, I know your heart is many a
time sad about Alick. He is far away and
there are others of us gone still farther, beyond the shores of this earth, whither our
poor thoughts vainly strive to follow them, —
our hearts' love following them still : — but
we know this one thing, that God is *there*

also, in America, in the dark Grave itself and
the unseen Eternity — even *He* is there too,
and will not He do all things well? We
have no other Anchor of the soul in any of
the tempests, great or little, of this world.
By this let us hold fast and piously hope in
all scenes and seasons whatsoever. Amen.

You bid me "call on Patience" in this
Book of mine. Dear Mother, it is the best
and only good advice that can be given. I do
endeavour to call on patience and sometimes
she comes, and if I keep my shoulder stiffly
at the wheel withal, we shall certainly get
under way by and bye. The thing goes indeed, or now promises to go, a little better
with me. I stand to it as I can. But it will
be a terribly difficult job and take a long
time, I think. However, that it is a useful
one, worthy to be done by me I am resolved,
and so I will do it if permitted — the return
and earthly reward of it may be either great
or small, or even nothing and abuse into the
bargain, just as it likes. Thank Heaven I
can do either or any way as to that, for this
time, and indeed, often when I look at it, the
prizes people get in this world and the kind
of people that get them seem but a *ridiculous*
business. If there were not something more

serious behind all that, I think it would hardly be worth while to live in such a place as this world at all. In short I hold on the best I can — and my good Mother's picture looking down on me here, seems to bid me " call on Patience " and persevere like a man.

Jane has not been very well in these cold stormy weeks, but I think is now getting better again. It is the spring weather, which this year has been the real winter ; all manner of people are unwell here at present. You in the North have it still worse, far worse than we. Many a time have I asked myself what is becoming of my good old Mother in these wild blasts. Surely you keep good fires at Scotsbrig ? Surely you wear the new Hawick sloughs ? Jane finds hers very warm and nice ; but the thing you might improve greatly and never do is your *diet*. I think you should live chiefly on fowl. A hen is always fair food, divide her into four pieces — she makes you an excellent dinner of soup and meat for four days. This you know very well for others, but never learn it for your-self. I am very serious. You *should* actu-ally set about this reform. Do now — you will find it more important on your health than any medicine or other appliance you can

think of. Jenny, I suppose, is still at the
Gill. When you feel tired of solitude again
she will come back to you. The bairns as
they grow will be quieter and give less trouble. Poor Jenny, no doubt of it, she has
many cares of her own: we should all be
gentle with her, pity her and help her what
we can.

But now I suppose you are very impatient
to know what is in that paste board roll tied
with string. Open the string with your scis-
sors and you will see — one of the ugliest
pictures ever drawn of man. A certain person here has been publishing some book
called " Spirit of the Age," pretending to
give people account of all the remarkable men
of the age; he has put me into it — better
luck to him. He wrote several months ago
requesting that I should furnish him with
some life of myself — forsooth ! This I altogether begged leave respectfully to decline,
but he got hold of a picture that a certain
painter has of me, and of this he has made
an engraving, — like *me* in nothing, or in
very little, I should flatter myself. Let Isabella roll the paper of it the *contrary way*
and then it will lie flat, if indeed the post
office bags do not squeeze it all to pieces,

which I think is fully as likely and will be no great matter. I sent it to you as to the one that had a right to it. Much good may it do you!

Jamie said he would write. Let him do so — or else you yourself ought to write, or *both* will be best. Jack and I were at Dinner together among a set of notables the night before last, came home together smoking two cigars, all right. Adieu, dear Mother, my big sheet is done. My regards to Isabella, to Jamie and them all. My blessings with you, dear Mother.

Yours affect.

T. CARLYLE.

Carlyle maps the Gill, as well as other places to which these letters make frequent reference, in his introductory note to Letter 283, in the " Letters and Memorials of Jane Welsh Carlyle : " — " The Gill, Sister Mary's poor but ever kind and generous *human* habitation, is a small farmhouse, seven miles beyond Annan, twenty-seven beyond Carlisle, eight or ten miles short of Dumfries. . . . Scotsbrig lies some ten miles northward of the Gill (road at right angles to the Carlisle and Dumfries Railway)."

"Our brother," spoken of in the second paragraph, is again the half-brother already mentioned.

XXX. CARLYLE TO MRS. JAMES AUSTIN, THE GILL.

CHELSEA, 30*th April*, 1844.

MY DEAR MARY, — We seldom hear directly of you and it is a long while since you have had an express word from any of our hands here. You are not to suppose that we forget you on that account. Far enough from that! You are many times in my thoughts. I fancy you and James struggling along in your diligent, industrious way, struggling to fight your battles in these bad times, and from the bottom of my heart I affectionately bid you God Speed. Struggle away, my dear sister. We must so struggle and we must not be beaten. Assure yourself always that I am not less brother-like in heart towards you than in old days when you saw me oftener and heard from me oftener. To-day I send you a little slip of paper which will turn into a sovereign when you present it at the Annan Post Office and sign your name "Mary Austin" — from me "at Chelsea." If you be not there yourself, James can sign for you if you sign it first, but the thing is

in no haste and will lie till you go. Buy
yourself a bit of a bonnet or anything you
like with the piece of money and wear it with
my blessing, sometimes thinking of us here.

No doubt you hear duly about us. You
have heard I suppose how Alick is gone over
to Canada, to our brother there, not into the
deep Western regions of America with Clow,
which Canada arrangement of Alick's we like
better than the other. It seems to me Alick
may do well there now. He will get a piece
of land and every year that he tills it faithfully it will be growing better for him. Labour is labour, not joyful but heavy and sore
in any part of this world, but if a person see
any fruit of his labour it is always an encour-
agement to him.

Our dear old Mother seems to have been
rather weaklier this last winter than heretofore. Jack had a letter yesterday from Jen-
nie at Scotsbrig which represents her as being
pretty well at present. I think Jenny should
stay much with her and look after her. Good
old Mother — the spring weather will grow
gradually into steady summer and then she
will have a better time of it, we may hope.

Jack was here last night. He talks of going North to " the country," probably toward

Annandale, before long, but his movements are very uncertain. He has not yet any fixed employment here and would be much better if he had. He does not seem to like medicine and is hovering among a great variety of things. We always hope he will fix himself on some specific object by and bye. As for me I am very busy but making very bad progress. I have nothing for it but to *bore* along mole-like ; I shall get out some time or other. Our spring wind has turned round tempestuously into the North of late and brought cold and dust, with the glare of sunshine, not so pleasant to the invalid part of us. Jane, however, is tolerably well and growing stronger as the sun grows. She sends her old love to you and kind remembrances. Give my regards to James — he must be planting his potatoes now. Love to you.

John Sterling, whose illness is lamented in the next letter, died on the 18th of the following September. Shortly before his death he wrote to Carlyle : " Towards me, it is still more true than towards England, that no man has been and done like you."

CHELSEA, *5th Aug.* 1841.

MY DEAR BROTHER, — Your letter in my
dearth of news was very welcome to me.
You should keep me going at least for Scotsbrig news while you are there. Our good
Mother must go back to the bathing. I hope
the next spring, rides will prove handier.
Our weather here too is much broken with
rain, though otherwise warm and genial.

I asked about your Book-sheets of Coch-
rane. The sheets were duly furnished : the
book is lying bound and ready in the London
Library. I would have brought it home with
me had there been a conveyance at my command. I left it lying there for yourself. Our
City is got almost empty and very quiet in
comparison. I hope I shall get on with somewhat less interruption in my labour; it is a
sluggish element, sluggish as thick mud and
bottomless, except when one *makes* a bottom.
Nothing but strenuous hard work, harder
than I have yet continuously given it, will
ever bring me through; for all is chaos
within it and without it. Eheu !

A striving Scotch youth came to me the
other week, equal, as he said, to all kinds of

old manuscripts &c, &c. I gave him a sovereign to copy me that Election Tumult? of d'Ewer at Ipswich. I have got that here and think of trying to make a magazine article of it somewhere. The poor lad attempted farther to make an estimate of copying all d'Ewer's Parl't manuscript for me. £30, he said, would do it and I had for some days real thoughts of the thing, but alas, my man in the interim was discovered by me to be a quite loose-talking, dishonest-minded little thing, unable to employ on any business; so having found him a job with Maurice, writing to dictation (in which dishonesty cannot long remain undetected) I shook him off, but it does partly appear to me I must have that MSS. to read and con over at my leisure — if possible. I am now about consulting with the Secretary of the Camden Society, but expect to hear that they, poor dilettante quacks, will do nothing. Nothing however will serve me as an answer from *them*. I think if I had the MS. right here I could either now or some time pay myself £30 of it. On the whole I am looking out for a hand amanuensis to copy me a good many things. I find such a one may be got, if you alight luckily, for some £60 or £80 to work all the year round; it is but the price of keeping a horse here. On the other hand no Bookseller can be made in the least to bite at such a thing ; — the inane mountebank quacks, — one must do it one's self or it will remain undone. I made them get into the Library a Thrigg and now also a Vicen, Part First, which are real conquests to me.

Nothing remarkable has arrived here except Emerson's letter, which indeed is not very remarkable either. Poor Sterling, as you will see by it, and may know more directly now from me, continues very ill, even I begin now to doubt, to despond altogether. He is obliged to " sit up all night propped with pillows," the greater part of his lungs (Clark says) is quite useless to him and he cannot get breath enough without immense difficulty. Anthony is going down to wait near him awhile. Poor Sterling! I fear the worst. Robertson, they say, is in Sutherland, marking out the site of Free Kirks. Go ahead!

Jamie's letter was very gratifying and satisfactory ; certainly we will take a couple more of Annandale hams. I will write to him more specially on the subject very soon.

Isabella too is in the way of shower baths
and better: Bravely that is good. Did any
of you write to Alick by this mail? Jane is
well again from her bit of headaches. Blessings on my Mother and you all.

T.

In 1844 there was "no Scotland" for Carlyle, but early in September he went to Mr.
and Lady Harriet Baring at the Grange.
The Baring friendship had begun to rise into
his life, — not yet in the form of a cloud.

All the rest of the year Carlyle stayed
closely at home, working on Cromwell, and
seeing fewer people than usual. The following quaint fragment belongs to this period,
from which Froude has preserved none of
Carlyle's letters or journal record.

XXXII. CARLYLE TO MRS. HANNING.

CHELSEA, 16*th Dec.* 1844.

DEAR JENNY, — I dare say you can knit
Wristikins. It has struck me in these cold
days I might as well apply to you to have a
pair. The best pair I yet have is a very old
pair now, which either you, or I think Jean,

knit for me at Hoddam Hill when you were little bairns many years ago. They have beautiful stripes of *red* yet, as fresh as ever. In fact I sometimes wear them in preference to the pair Jane has bought for me out of the shops here. Being already provided as you see I will not in the least hurry you as to the matter — wait till you have leisure, till you can get right your colors &c. &c. — only I will tell you what kind of thing will suit me and how you can do it when convenient. The great defect of all my present wristikins is that they are too slight, too *thin*, and do not fill up the cuff of the coat, which is rather wide with me. They should be at least *double* the common thickness of those in the shops. If you had fine, *boozy* yarn and took it *two ply* it will make a pretty article. Then as to color, it should be deep for our reeky atmosphere here; red is beautiful, a stripe of good red, and holds out well, but perhaps the basis had better be some sort of brown. Please your own eye. There never was a good horse had an *ill* color. As to breadth I think they should be at least three inches. . . .

The horse which Carlyle describes to his

mother as " a very darling article " was a new one, called " Black Duncan."

Of Addiscombe Froude writes : " The Barings had a villa at Addiscombe, and during the London season frequently escaped into the Surrey sunshine."

XXXIII. CARLYLE TO HIS MOTHER, SCOTSBRIG.

CHELSEA, 12*th July*, 1845.

MY DEAR MOTHER, — My hurry is indeed great, but it ought to be greater than it is before I neglect writing you a little word *this* week as I did last. I am whipt about from post to pillar at a strange rate in these weeks.

Jack's visit to you was a welcome piece of news here. The good account he gave of you was much wanted. We are very sorry indeed to hear of poor Isabella. It seems as if nothing could be done for her, and her own weakness and suffering must be very great. Jamie is kind and patient, you may assure him of our sympathies. A sudden turn for the better may take place, I understand, as of its own accord all at once. Let us keep hoping the best.

The back of this sorrowful Book is now broken. I think another month of stiff labour will see it well through. They are printing

away at the second volume — about half
done. I have to go along amid endless confusions. the way one has to do in all work
whatsoever. The Book will, on the whole,
be better than I hoped, and I have had some
honest thoughts in the writing of it which
make me the more careless what kind of reception the world gives it. The world had
better try to understand it, I think, and to
like it as well as it can! Here is another leaf
of a proof sheet to be a token to you of our
progress. So soon as ever it is over I am off
for Annandale. The heat has never been
very oppressive to me, never violent beyond a
day or two at a time, then rain comes and
cools it again. I get considerable benefit of
my horse, which is a very darling article,
black, high, very good natured, very swift —
and takes me out into the green country for
a taste of that almost every day. I sometimes think of *riding* it up into Annandale,
but that will be too lengthy an operation.

Jane is going to Liverpool to her Uncle's
in a fortnight. She will stay with them a
week, then another week with some country
friends in that quarter. I wished her to
go to Scotland and see old friends there at
Haddington and elsewhere, but she is rather

reluctant to that. She is not very strong
and has many sorrows of her own, poor little
thing, being very solitary in the world now.
In summer however she is always better.

I have heard nothing from Jack of late
days. I suppose him to be still at Mr.
Raine's. Perhaps uncertain whitherward he
will go next. At any rate country is better
than town at present, — free quarter than
board-wages. I expect he will come back to
you again before the season end.

We were out at a place called Addiscombe
last week among great people, very kind to us,
but poor Jane could sleep only about an hour
each night — three hours in all. I stayed
but one night, came home on my black horse
again. Some peace and rest among green
things would be very welcome to me — and it
is coming soon, I hope. Adieu, dear Mother
— my kind love to you and to all of them. I
am in great haste and can speak but a few
words to mean much by them. My blessings
with you.

On the 26th August, 1845, Carlyle wrote:
" I have this moment *ended* Oliver ; hang it !
He is ended, thrums and all." And presently

the author joined his wife at Seaforth near
Liverpool.   After a few days there with the
Paulets, he went on by water to Annan and
his mother.   From Seaforth again, he writes
to her on the journey Chelsea-ward.

XXXIV. CARLYLE TO HIS MOTHER, SCOTSBRIG.

SEAFORTH, LIVERPOOL,
Friday, 17 *Oct'r*, 1845.

MY DEAR MOTHER, — I hope you have,
this morning, got the little Note I pushed
into the Post Office for you at Lancaster, and
consoled yourself with the assurance that all
the difficult part of my journey was well over.
I am quite safe, and in good quarters here,
since yesterday afternoon; and will now write
you another word with a little more delibera-
tion than yesterday.   My journey hither was
altogether really pleasant: a fine bright day,
and a swift smooth carriage to sit in, nothing
wanted that one could wish on such an occasion.   I got along to this house about half
past four, when dinner was ready and a welcome as if it had been home, — real joy to
me.   It has all gone much better than I could
have expected since I quitted Kirtlebrig and
Jamie, that night.

I find the good people here *did* send their

carriage for the Steamer; and a very wild adventure that was, and much better that *I* had but little to do with it, and could plead that I had forbidden them to do such a thing! The Paulet carriage went duly to the Clarence Dock, after inquiring at the Steamer Office too, and waited for the Royal Victoria from half past 8 on Wednesday night till past 12, when the Docks *close;* but no Royal Victoria came! She did not make her appearance till noon *yesterday,* owing to fog or wind, or what cause I have not yet heard, — not till twelve o'clock yesterday; when the Paulet carriage was again in attendance: but of course there was no guest there; the guest was advancing by another much less uncomfortable route! On the whole it was a good luck I did not get into that greasy Whale's Belly (as I call it); twenty-four hours there would have reduced me to a precious pickle!

Our journey to Lancaster as I told you was decidedly prosperous, almost pleasant thro' the moonlight country, with plenty tobacco to smoke! The wild solitude of Shap Fell at midnight is a thing I really like to have seen. And then the railway yesterday was all the welcomer, and the daylight. At

Carlisle I got myself a pound of tobacco from Irving, so do not fret your heart, dear Mother, about that! I also took out my old dressing-gown there and wrapt it well round my legs, which was useful. A small proportion of corn, you may tell Jamie, was still in the fields here and there all the way; but to-day and last night there is a rustling *thuddening* North wind which must have dried it.

Dr. Carlyle's Dante, which he was very "eager upon," was the prose translation of the Inferno, so well done that many readers have regretted that the translator did not proceed.

XXXV. CARLYLE TO HIS MOTHER. SCOTSBRIG.

CHELSEA, 31 *Oct'r*, 1843.

MY DEAR MOTHER, — You will take a short word from me rather than none at all, to tell you that we are all struggling along here without disaster; which indeed is all that is to be told. I write also to see if I can induce you to make use of one of those Letter-covers which I left, and to send me a small line about yourself and how you are. Except one short line from Jamie to the Doctor, I have heard nothing at all since I left you.

There has been no rain, or almost none whatever since I left Scotsbrig; so that, I hope, tho' your weather can hardly have been so favourable, Jamie is now over with his harvest, and fast getting all secured under *thatch-and-rope*. The Potatoe business, as I learn from the Newspapers, proves very serious everywhere, in Ireland as much as anywhere; and over all Europe there is a rather deficient crop; besides which, the present distracted railway speculation and general fever of trade is nearly certain to break down soon into deep confusion, so that one may fear a bad winter for the poor, a sad thing to look forward to. They are best off, I think, who have least to do with that brutal Chase for money which afflicts me wherever I go in this country. " Give me neither poverty nor riches, feed me with food convenient for me."

Our freedom from rain has not hindered the November fogs from coming in somewhat before their time. The weather is not wholesome, many people have got cold in these late days. I advise you, dear Mother, to put on your winter clothing and be cautious of going out except when the sun is shining. In the morning and evening do not venture

at all. This is the most critical time of all,
I believe, these weeks while the change to
winter is just in progress. I thought myself
extremely well here for a week after my return, and indeed was so and hope again to be
so — much improved by my journey, — but
last Sabbath, paying no heed to these frost
fogs, I caught a little tickling in my nose
which rapidly grew into a *sniftering*, and by
the time next day came I had a regular ugly
face-ache and fair foundation for cold in all
its forms, which required to be energetically
dealt with and resisted on the threshold.
Next day, accordingly, I kept the house
strictly and appealed to medicine and their
diet, and so on Wednesday morning I had
got the victory again and have been getting
round and growing nearer the old point ever
since — in fact reckon myself quite well again,
except that I take a little care of going out
at night &c. Jane has had a little whiff of
cold too, but it is abating again. We are
taught by these visitations to be upon our
guard. The Doctor is quite well, tho' I
think he sits too much in the house, being
very eager upon his Dante at present.

They are not to publish the Cromwell till
" the middle of next month " — about a fortnight.

" They are not to publish the Cromwell till
' the middle of next month,' " wrote Carlyle in
the preceding letter. As a matter of fact the
book did not get out until December.

Carlyle and his wife did go to the Barings
in the middle of November, and the date of
the following undated fragment thus swings
between the 1st and the 15th of November.
Carlyle says here that they were invited to the
Grange ; Froude, that Mr. Baring and Lady
Harriet were at Bay House, in Hampshire.
" Grange " is probably a slip of the pen.

XXXVI. CARLYLE TO HIS MOTHER, SCOTSBRIG.

CHELSEA [1/15 *November*, 1845].

. . . It lies perfectly ready, but the Town
is still very empty ; besides they are getting
ready a Portrait, the *rudiments* of which
John and I went to see the other day, but
did not very much like. I fear it will not
turn out much of an ornament to the Book
or a *true* likeness of Oliver ; but we cannot
help that. Nor does it very much matter. —
For the rest, I am and have been nearly as
idle as possible ; merely reading Books, and
doing other small etceteras.

There is an invitation to go down to the
Grange (where I was the other year), for

Jane and me both, " for a few days " (perhaps three) ; but I think it is not certain whether we can accept in such a state of the weather, etc. It will be within the next ten days if at all. We are very quiet here at home ; hardly anybody yet coming about us : and indeed in general it is, the fewer the better, with us.

I cannot yet learn with the least distinctness whether John is for Scotsbrig or not ; but I continue to think he will after all come down and plant himself there with his *Dante* for a while. I have fully expressed your wishes to him in regard to that ; and certainly if he do not come it will not be for want of wish to be there.

Jenny, I suppose, is home again : all is grown quiet in the upstairs rooms ! My dear good Mother, let us not be sad, let us rather be thankful, — and still hope in the Bounty which has long been so benignant to us. I will long remember your goodness to me at Scotsbrig on this occasion, and the sadness that is in it I will take as inevitable, — every joy has its sorrow here. . . .

If I think of any Carlisle Tobacco I will send word about it in good time; if I send no word, do not in the least delay about it.

" In February, 1846," says Froude, " a new edition was needed of the Cromwell. Fresh letters of Oliver had been sent which required to be inserted according to date; a process, Carlyle said, ' requiring one's most excellent talent, as of shoe-cobbling, really that kind of talent carried to a high pitch.'

" He had 'to unhoop his tub, which already held water,' as he sorrowfully put his case to Mr. Erskine, ' and insert new staves.' "

Other editors of letters, before and since, have had such cobbling and coopering to do.

XXXVII. CARLYLE TO MRS. HANNING, DUMFRIES.

CHELSEA, Monday, 29*th June*, 1846.

DEAR JENNY, — I heard of your arrival in your new place at Dumfries a day or two ago, and on Saturday I sent you a newspaper which I suppose you will receive this morning. You will understand it as a hasty token that we are in our usual way and still mindful of you, although there has been little express writing of late.

No doubt you will feel a little lonely, unaccustomed, and now and then dispirited and anxious in your new situation. Yet I do consider it a very fit change for you to have made, and believe confidently you will find yourself

much more comfortable than you have been
in your old place, if once you are fairly *hafted*
to the new one.   Do not be discouraged, my
little Jenny, I know you will behave always in
a *douce*, prudent, industrious and wise way,
and there is no fear of you, if so.   You will
be mistress of your own little heart at any
rate, free to follow your own wisest purposes.
I think you will gradually find work, too,
which may be useful to you.   In short this is
a fact always, in Maxwell-town and in all towns
and situations, — a person that does act wisely
will find wise and good results following him
in this world and in all worlds; which really
is the comfort of poor struggling creatures
here below.   And I hope you understand
firmly always that you have friends who will
never forsake you, whom all considerations
bind to help you what they can, in the honest
fight you are making.   So do not fear, my
poor little sister; be wise and true and diligent and do the *best* you can, and it shall all
be well yet, and better than we hope.

Getting into a new house, it strikes me, you
must find various things defective and not yet
in order, so you must take this bit of paper
from me which James Aitken, on Wednesday
first, will change into three sovereigns for you

—and you must lay them out in furnitures and bits of equipments such as you see need-fullest. I know nobody that could lay them out better and make more advantage of them than you will do, only you want to consider that this is a supernumerary thing, a clear *gift*, and that your regular income (which John said was to be enlarged — whatever he may have settled it) will arrive at the usual time inde-pendently of this. And so, my blessing with you, dear little Jenny, and right good days to you in this new dwelling, — right *wise* days, which are the only good ones.

I have owed Jean a letter this long time. Tell her a box of supplements to Cromwell (one for each of you and two new copies of the whole book — one for my mother, the other for Jack) will reach her in a day or two, which she will know how to dispose of. For the rest, I am fast getting through my book, — it is mere *tatters* of work now, — and ex-pect to be off northward before long. *North-ward* we do mean; Jane sometimes talks of being off this week and I to follow in a week or two. To Seaforth, Liverpool, is Jane's first place. I, of course, will soon be across if once there. Good be with you, dear sister.

Yours always,   T. C.

Do *you* address the next newspaper to us if
this come all right.   That will be a sufficient
sign to us.

Chelsea, Saturday, 17*th October*, 1846.

Dear Sister, — That letter for the Doctor
reached me last night with instructions, as you
see, to forward it to you.   There is another
little one from poor little Jane, which I like
still better, but I am ordered to return it to
my mother.   Alick is going on very tolerably
and seems to do as well as one could expect in
his new settlement, — somewhat bitter of temper yet, but diligent and favoured to see the
fruits of his diligence.

We are extremely quiet here, not writing,
or expressly meditating to write, *resting* in
fact, for I find Chelsea greatly the quietest
place I could meet with.   This long while I
read a great many books of very little value,
see almost nobody except with the *eye* merely,
find silence better than speech — sleep better
than waking!   My thoughts are very *serious*,
I will not call them sorrowful or miserable; I
am getting fairly *old* and do not want to be
younger — I know not whether Jeffrey would
call that " happy " or not.

Our maid Helen is leaving us, invited to be some Housekeeper to a brother she has in Dublin, at present a rich trader there, "all upon float" as I sometimes fear. Jane is busy negotiating about a successor, hopes to get a suitable one from Edinburgh or almost to *have* got such. You have not written to me. Tell Jenny I will send her some word soon. My kind regards to James. Good be with you and your house, dear Jean. Jane is *out*, and therefore silent.

Ever yours,   T. C.

Between 1846 and the spring of 1849 Carlyle had made the acquaintance of Louis Blanc, John and Jacob Bright, and Sir Robert Peel.

On the 30th of June, 1849, Carlyle started on a journey through Ireland, — the notes of which were printed after his death, — and returned on the 7th of August. He went directly to Scotsbrig, where, " owing to cocks and other blessed fellow-inhabitants of this planet," he was a good deal disquieted. In Scotsbrig he remained, however, till the end of August.

XXXIX. CARLYLE TO MRS. HANNING, DUMFRIES.

SCOTSBRIG, 18 *August*, 1849.

DEAR SISTER JENNY, — Here is a Draft for
your money, which you will get by presenting
that Paper at the Bank, when the Martinmas
Term comes; I wish you much health and
good industrious days till the 22nd comes
round *again;* and have done nothing more
gladly, I may say, in the payment line than
write this little paper for you, ever since the
last was written, I think. It gave me very
great pleasure to see your neat little Lodging
and thrifty, modest, and wise way of life, when
we were in Dumfries the other day. The reports of all friends agree in testifying to the
same effect. Continue so, my good little sister,
and fear nothing that can befall. Our outward fortune, lucky or what is called unlucky,
we cannot command; but we *can* command
our own behaviour under it, and we do either
wisely or else not wisely; and *that*, in real
truth, makes *all* the difference, — and does in
reality stamp us as either "lucky" or else "unlucky." For there is nobody but he that acts
foolishly and *wrong* that can, in the end, be
called "unlucky;" he that acts wisely and
right is, before all mortals, to be accounted

"lucky;" he and no other than he. So toil honestly along, my dear little Jenny, even as heretofore; and keep up your heart. An elder brother's duty to you, I trust I may promise, you shall never stand in want of while I live in this world.

Take the next *Courier* (which Jean will give you for the purpose) and address it in your own hand to me: "Care of John Fergus, M. P. etc., Kirkcaldy," — or in fact if James Aitken write that, it will be all the same, — and I shall need no other sign that you have received this Note and Inclosure safe. You can tell James to send only one *Courier* that way; but to direct the other to Scotsbrig till further notice.

Our Mother and I got well home on Thursday; the thunder-showers hung and fell heavy on all hands of us; but we escaped with little damage from them, — got no rain at all till we were on the top of Dodbeck (or rather Daneby) Banks; which rain was never violent upon *us*, and had as good as ended altogether by the time we reached the old Gildha Road. Our Mother's new bonnet, or any of her clothes, suffered nothing whatever. There had *been* great rains here and all the way; the fields all running brooks, and the

road-conduits hardly able to contain the loads
they had.   It was a good deal clearer yesterday ; yet, in the evening, we had again a
touch of rain, which I saw was very heavy
over in Cumberland.   To-day is a degree
brisker still, tho' with remnants of thunder-
clouds still hanging, so we fancy the " Flood "
is about terminating, and the broken weather
going to heal itself again.   Jamie has some
cattle rather suffering by the " epidemic,"
which, in the last year, has destroyed several ;
his bog-hay, too, is of course much wetted ;
but he is otherwise getting briskly enough
along.   You are to tell James Aitken that
there is " an excellent spigot " here already
for the water-barrel, so that he need take no
farther heed of that, at least, till he hear
again.

I could not quite handily get packed (owing
to Garthwaites tailoring) for this day ; so I
put it off till Monday ; and am fixed for that
morning (10 A. M.) to be in Edinburgh about
one o'clock and over in Kirkcaldy in good
time, where Jane, as I conclude, is arrived
since yesterday and expects me against the
given time.   Give my kindest remembrances
in Assembly Street ; what our further movements from Kirkcaldy are to be, Jean or some

of you will hear in due time. No more at present, dear Sister, with many blessings to you all.

Ever your Affectionate Brother,
T. CARLYLE.

In 1850 the Latter-Day Pamphlets were published. In spite of the outcry against them, Carlyle's regular "public" was not disturbed. Froude estimates that about three thousand persons were then buying whatever Carlyle printed.

He wrote in his Journal during October of the same year: " Four weeks (September) at Scotsbrig : my dear old Mother, much broken since I had last seen her, was a perpetual source of sad and, as it were, sacred emotion to me. Sorrowful mostly and disgusting, and even degrading, were my other emotions. God help me ! "

The next letter concerns the departure of Mrs. Hanning to join her husband in Canada. It is the only one in this collection from Mrs. Thomas Carlyle. " Jane " is Carlyle's sister, Jean Aitken, — Jane only by courtesy, he somewhere says.

XL. MRS. THOMAS CARLYLE TO MRS. HANNING, DUMFRIES.

5 Cheyne Row, Tuesday [spring of 1851].

My dear Jenny, — I sent off yesterday by
railway to Jane's care a bundle of things
which I hope may be of some use to you in
your preparation for departure. They are
not much worth as they are, but you have a
great talent — at least you had when I knew
you — for making silk purses out of sows'
ears, a very valuable talent in this world. For
the rest what can I say to you but that I
wish you good speed in your great adventure,
and that it may turn out even better for you
than you hope. Decidedly it is an adventure
in which you ought to be let please yourself,
to be let follow the guidance of your own
heart without remonstrance or criticism of
others. It is my fixed opinion that between
man and wife no third person *can* judge, and
that all any of us could reasonably require of
you is that you should consider well what
you are about to do and that you should do
nothing from *secondary motives*. If it be
affection for your husband and the idea of
doing your duty by him that takes you from
your family and friends so far away, then go
in God's name, and may your husband prove

JANE WELSH CARLYLE

himself worthy of so much constancy. In any case you will have no cause for self-reproach. But if it be impatience of your position here which is driving you away from your kind old Mother and all the rest who love you so well, then God help you, my poor Jenny, for you are flinging away all the real blessings of your lot for an imagination of independence. I hope, however, you are quite justified by your feelings towards your husband in leaving all to follow him. You have always seemed to me to cherish a most loyal affection for your husband, and I will never believe, however appearances may be against him, that a man can inspire such an affection in the wife he has lived years beside and yet be wholly unworthy of it. So farewell, dear Jenny, and God go with you.

Affectionately yours,

JANE CARLYLE.

Three months of the late winter and early spring of 1851 had sufficed for writing the life of John Sterling. Julius Hare and the religious newspapers had treated Sterling as a poor stray lamb from the Christian fold. Hare regarded him as "a vanquished doubter;" Carlyle, as "a victorious believer."

"Here, visible to myself for some while," wrote he, "was a brilliant human presence, distinguishable, honourable, and loveable amid the dim common populations, among the million little beautiful once more a beautiful human soul, whom I among others recognised and lovingly walked with while the years and the hours were." Carlyle's life of the man whom he thus looked upon came out like a star after the storm of the "Latter-Day Pamphlets." Full of a kind of shining peace, the work of an artist perturbed by neither controversy nor any need of "buffeting his books," the Life of Sterling is one of the very few most beautiful biographies in English.

XLI. JOHN AITKEN CARLYLE TO MRS. HANNING, HAMILTON.

Scotsbrig, 27 *June*, 1851.

My dear Jenny, — Mr. Smellie wrote punctually to tell us you had sailed on the 27th of last month exactly according to appointment, and that he had seen you on the day following some twelve miles down the Clyde, having gone to give you a Brooch you had forgotten in his mother's house. He said your berths looked very comfortable, and spoke of the Clutha as a tight good ship, every way fit for the voyage. Almost every day since that time we have had westerly winds, and if you have had the same, your voyage is likely to be considerably longer than you anticipated. I hardly know whether to write by this week's post, or wait till next, but it seems best to err on the safe side, for you will expect to find a letter at Hamilton whenever you arrive, and be much disappointed if there be none. My writing need not be otherwise than briefly, as we are all going on in much the same way as when you left us. Our Mother has been uneasy whenever the winds were sounding loud, and once or twice she has taken to bed, but she is now at least as strong as usual and moving about in the old way. She desires me to send her love to yourself and the children, and kindest regards to your husband, and bids you write without delay whenever you get to your home in the far West. We had a note from Dumfries two days ago, Jean and hers are all well, James as busy as possible with one thing and another. We expect them here next week, and hope Jean will remain a few days. Mary was here on Tuesday last. She is looking stouter than usual and things seem to be a little more prosperous at the Gill than they have been of late years. I was there very lately along with Jamie, who went to purchase some cattle. From Chelsea we heard yesterday. Tom is busy with his Life of J. Sterling, which is now going through the press. He has not yet decided whether we are to expect him here or not this season. There is one of the Miss Welsh's of Liverpool staying with them at Cheyne Row.

Little Jamie takes this with him to Annan. I need not add any more except to mention that Mr. Goold had received a letter from your husband to you addressed to his care, a short time after you sailed. I will send you a paper now and then with its *two* strokes if we continue all well.

Our Mother sent a copy of the second edition of Cromwell's Letters to Mr. Smellie, the week after you sailed, and had an acknowledgement from him. She wished him to have some memorial from her, for all his kindness to you in looking after your berths, etc., etc.

Ever yours affectionately,
J. A. CARLYLE.

The following letter, interesting as it is,

jars a little on the homely calm of the series. The Exhibition and the "glass palace" need no explanation. Church and State are still English facts.

XLII. CARLYLE TO ALEXANDER CARLYLE, CANADA.

CHELSEA, 24 *Oct'r*, 1851.

MY DEAR BROTHER, — About a fortnight ago I wrote to you intimating that I would soon send a copy of a Book called Life of John Sterling, which was just about coming out, and also that I would write soon again. Last week, in good time for the mail, said Life of Sterling did accordingly set out towards you. On enquiring practically I found such a feat was now quite handy. If the Book weighs *under* one pound, it will go to Canada or from it for a shilling; if under two pounds and above one, you must pay two shillings, (in *stamps* always), and so on for other weights. It is an immense convenience and I design if I live to make use of it on other occasions on your behalf. If all went right the book will reach you about a week before this present letter, if it do *not*, write to me and I will take some order in the matter. If it do come rightly you may send me an old newspaper addressed in your hand.

That will be announcement enough for the purpose, and so we have finished this affair of the Book, let us hope.

Since I wrote last our "Exhibition" has dissolved itself, all gone or going to the four winds, and on our streets there is a blessed tranquillity in comparison. London is of all the year stillest at this season or a little earlier. All one's acquaintances are in the country, two or three hundred thousand of the inhabitants are in the country. Now is the time for a little *study*, for a little private meditation and real converse with one's self —a thing not to be neglected, however little pleasant it be. The days are getting foggy, a kind of dusky, *stoory*-looking, dry fog, dimmed with much thin reek over and above, not an exhilarating element at all, but it is very quiet comparatively and one ought to be thankful. I often think I will go into the country to live, *out* of this dirty reek and noise, but I am very *feckless* for making changes and find all countries (Annandale itself) grown very solitary and questionable to me. "Busy, busy, be busy with thy work :" — let that in the meanwhile suffice as commandment for me.

Within the week I have news from Scotsbrig. Our dear old Mother was reported well (for her) " better than when I was there." Jack being now with her, that is always a considerable fact in her favor. The good old woman, she can do wonderfully when things go perfectly "straight," but a small matter is now sufficient to over-set her. She can *read*, the whole day if she have any Book worth reading, and her appetite for reading is not at all sickly or squeamish, but can eagerly welcome almost anything that has, on any subject, a glimmering of human sense in it. Jamie's harvest is well over, a rather superior crop for *quality*, the quantity about an average, that is the account he gives — and indeed it is the general account of the country this year. Trade is good this year or more back ; so that numbers of the people are or might be well off (tho' I think they mainly *waste* their superior wages) and huge multitudes of vagrant, distressed wretches are to be found everywhere even now. What will there be when " trade," as it soon will do, takes another turn. Strolling Irish, hawk- ing, begging, doing all kinds of coarse labour, are getting daily more abundant — unhappy beings ! We hear from the Newspapers much absurd talk about the " Millions that have emigrated to America." Alas, it has been to England and Scotland that they have "emigrated." as anybody but a Stump Orator or Newspaper Editor might see — and they will produce their effects here by and by! — On the whole, dear Brother, you are right happy to have got out of this horrible welter into a quiet garden of your own over the sea. There are times coming here, and rushing on with ever faster speed, though unnoticed by the "glass palace" sages and their followers, such as none of us have ever seen for violence and misery. Church and State and all the arrangements of a rotten society, often seem to me as if they were not worth 20 years' purchase and the thing that will first follow them is nearly certain to be greatly *worse* than they. God mend it. We can do nothing for it but try if possible to mind our own work in the middle of it.

There came a letter lately from Sister Jenny which reports of you at Bield in a very interesting and cheering fashion. You are not much changed except (like myself) a little whiter in the *happits*. Tom is a stout handy looking fellow, not too tall. Jane a douce tidy lass, in short "you look all very comfortable on your two farms." We were thankful enough for such a pictorial report, I need not tell you. As to Jenny herself there seem good omens too, and we hope her husband and she may now do well, *his* follies having stilled themselves with advance of years. At all events she will be more content than in Dumfries in her old position : there it was clear enough she could not abide much longer. That she is near you on any emergency is a great comfort to our Mother and the rest of us.

Adieu, dear Brother, I did not mean to write so much to-day, being hurried enough with many things. Jane sends her love to her namesake and to you all. I wish you would buy Tom an American copy of one of my books, (Translation of W. Meister? No?), and give it him as a memento of me and you, some time when his behaviour is at the best. Assure him, at any rate, of my hearty regard, him and all the household. My blessing with you all.

Affectionately,
T. CARLYLE.

By 1851 Carlyle had begun to think seriously of Frederick the Great as his next subject, and it soon became evident that he must walk in whatever footsteps of his hero were still visible. Carlyle reached Rotterdam September 1, 1852, at noon, and was there met by Mr. Neuberg, — "a German admirer," says Froude, " a gentleman of good private fortune, resident in London, who had volunteered his services to conduct Carlyle over the Fatherland, and afterwards to be his faithful assistant in the ' Frederick ' biography." Carlyle returned to England in October, but many distractions — among them repairs in Cheyne Row and the funeral of the Duke of Wellington — kept him from starting with Frederick. During the winter he wrote something, and threw it aside. On the 13th of April, 1853, he wrote in his Journal, " Still struggling and haggling about Frederick."

There is neither struggling nor haggling, however, in the letter which follows. The " Talbottypes " mentioned here were, like " Daguerreotypes," dim and glimmering prophecies of the merciless photograph.

XLIII. CARLYLE TO MRS. HANNING, CANADA.

5 CHEYNE ROW, CHELSEA, LONDON,
22 Apl. 1853.

MY DEAR JENNY, — Though it is a long

time since I have written to you, no mistake
can be greater than that I have forgotten
you. No, no, there is no danger of that.
My memory at least is active enough! But
I live in such a confused whirlpool of hurries
here as you can have no conception of, and
always in poor weak health, too, and in corresponding spirits, and for most part when
my poor stroke of work for the day is done
(if alas, I be lucky enough to get any work
done one day in ten, as days now go!) — I
have in general nothing for it but to shut
up my ugly cellar of confusions and address
myself to the task of being *silent* — writing no letter whatever but those I absolutely
cannot help. That is the real truth and
you must not measure my regard for you by
the quantity I write, but by quite other standard.

We regularly see your letters here and are
very glad indeed to observe that you get on
so well. The fits of ague-fever you had at
first were a severe introduction and began to
be alarming to us, but I can hope now it was
only the *hanselling* of you in your new climate, and that henceforth you will go on with
at least your old degree of health. One thing
I have understood to be of great moment

(indeed I am sure of it), in the Canada climate; it is to take good care that your house be in an airy situation, quite free from the neighbourhood of damp ground, especially of stagnant water, and with a free exposure to the wind. That undoubtedly is of great importance. You are accustomed from sound old Annandale to take no thought at all about such things, but you may depend upon it they are necessary and indispensable considerations in your new country. I beg you very much to keep them earnestly in view with reference to the house you live in. Plenty of dry wind, all marshes &c. at a distance, and there is no more danger of ague in Canada than in Scotland; that you shove up your windows in season and keep your house *clean* as a new pin — these are advices I need not give, for you follow these, of course, of nature or inveterate habit, being from of old one of the neatest little bodies to be found in five Parishes! In all remaining respects I find you have chosen clearly for the better, and I doubt not are far happier in your reunited household than you ever were or could have been in Dumfries. It was a wise and courageous adventure of you to take the Ocean by the face in search of these objects, and all your friends rejoice to learn that it has succeeded. Long and richly may you reap the rewards of your quiet, stout and wise behaviour — then and all along, under circumstances that were far from easy to manage; and God's blessing be on you always, my poor little Jenny! I hope, too, poor Robert has learned many a thing and forgotten many a thing in the course of his hard fortune and wide wanderings. Give him my best wishes, temporal and spiritual. *Help* him faithfully what you can, and he (for he has a kind enough heart) will do the like by you — and so we hope all will be better with you both than it is with many, and continue to grow better and better to the end. I recommend myself to the nice *gley* little lasses whom I shall not forget, but always think of as *little*, however *big* they grow. My blessing on you all.

No doubt you know by eyesight whom these two *Talbottypes* represent; mine is very like — Jane's (done by a different process) is not quite so like, but it will serve for remembrance. I begged two pairs of them awhile ago and had one sent to Alick (*Jane* slightly different in his set), the other pair I now send to you and wish only it were some *usefuller* gift. However, they will eat no bread and so you may give them dry lodging, that is all they want.

I heard from the Dr. at Moffat the day before yesterday. He reports our good old Mother being in her usual way and now with the better prospect of summer ahead. Poor Mother, she is now very feeble, but her mind is still all there and we should be thankful. The rest are well. John is to quit Moffat in July. Jane sends her kind regards.

The White mat on Jane's lap is her wretched little *messin*-dog " Nero ; " a very unsuccessful part of the drawing, that !

XLIV. CARLYLE TO MRS. HANNING. CANADA.

Scotsbrig, Ecclefechan, 28 *Dec.* 1853.

My dear Sister, — This letter brings very sorrowful news to you, probably the sorrowfullest I may ever have to send from Scotsbrig. Our dear and good old Mother is no more : she went from us, gently and calmly at last, on the Sunday just gone (Christmas Day the 25th) at four or ten minutes past four in the afternoon : The Dr., Jean, Isabella, Jamie, and I standing in sorrowful reverence at her bed-side ; our poor suffering Mother had lain in a heavy kind of sleep for about 16 hours before; and died at last, rather unexpectedly to the watchers, so sudden was it, without struggle or seeming pain of any kind. We had to think " Her sufferings are over; and she has fought her fight well and nobly; and as for us, — we are left here alone; and the soul that never ceased to love us since we came into the world, is gone to God, her Maker and ours." This is the heavy news I have to send you, dear Sister; and nobody can spare you the sorrow and tears it will occasion. For above a year-and-a-half past, our dear Mother had been visibly falling fast away; when I saw her in August gone a year, her weakness and sufferings were quite painful to me; and it seemed uncertain whether we should ever meet again in this scene of things. She had no disease at that time nor afterwards, but the springs of life were worn out, there was no strength left. Within the last six months the decay proceeded faster and was constant: she could not much rise from bed; she needed Mary and Jean alternately to watch always over her, — latterly it was Jean alone (Mary not being strong enough); and surely Jean has earned the gratitude of us all, and done a work that was blessed and beautiful, in so standing by her sacred task, and so performing it as she did. There has been no regular sleep to her for months past, often of late weeks and days not much sleep of any kind: but her affectionate patience, I think, never failed. I hope, though she is much worn out, she will not permanently suffer: and surely she will not want her reward. Our noble Mother too behaved like herself in all stages of her illness; never quailed into terror, lamentation or any weak temper of mind; had a wonderful clearness of intellect, clearness of heart, affection, piety and simple courage and beauty about her to the very end. She passed much of her time in the last weeks in a kind of sleep; used to awaken "with a smile" (as John described it to me), and has left a sacred remembrance with all of us consolatory in our natural grief.

I have written to Alick this day, a good many other details, and have bidden him send you the letter (which is larger and fuller than this), — as you probably in asking for it will send this to him. I am in great haste, to-morrow (Thursday 29th Dec.) being the funeral day, and many things occupying us still. I will therefore say no more here ; your little pieces of worldly *business* will, I hope, be satisfactorily and easily adjusted before I return to Chelsea, and then it will be somebody's task (John's or mine) to write to you again. For the present I will only bid, God bless you, dear sister, you and yours; — and teach you to bear this great sorrow and bereavement (which is one chiefly to your heart, but to *her* a blessed relief) in the way that is fit, and worthy of the brave and noble Mother we have had, but have not any longer.

Your affectionate Brother,
T. CARLYLE.

With a few days excepted, the Carlyles spent the whole of the year 1854 in London. There was little but the Crimean war to distract Carlyle's attention from his long struggle with Frederick.

Early in this year was completed the much talked of " sound-proof room," of which the best account is given by Mr. Reginald Blunt, in his little-known book, "The Carlyles' Chelsea Home."

" The arrangement of this room, which was built in 1853, occupied by Carlyle till 1865, and afterwards used as a servant's bedroom, is clearly indicated on the plan ; whilst Mr.

Tait's photographs (taken in 1857) give an excellent record of its aspect. Indeed, it is not often that so famous a literary workshop has been so faithfully depicted for posterity. The spacious skylight, which drove Carlyle to despair by besmutting his books and papers, gave his visitor the abundant light which indoor photography so often lacks, and the result is a series of pictures of wonderful interest. Mr. Tait was good enough to intrust the negatives to me to make my own prints; and it was, indeed, a fascinating employment to resuscitate, by a few minutes of exposure to light, these speaking records of the dead past of nearly forty years ago. By their aid we have little difficulty in mentally reconstituting the ' soundless room ' as it was during Carlyle's ' thirteen years' war ' there. Entering by the door at the head of the staircase (a second door opens into the cupboard space, though for what reason, unless to provide a means of escape, is not obvious), one finds immediately to one's right hand a third door into this same closet. Beyond it, against the partition wall, stood a half-round table with an oilcloth cover, carrying books and papers; above it hung a small portrait of Carlyle's mother, an engraving of

Frederick on horseback, and a map, pinned on the wall, unframed. On the north wall, to the right of the fireplace, shelved cupboards were fitted. Over the square white marble mantelpiece, with its 'merely human' fireplace and white-tiled sides, hung several small sketches and engravings around the wooden pulley-board, to which were attached the lines for the sliding-shutter and the ventilators. On the left of the fire, above a circular silk-pleated screen, hung a paper rack and some written notes on Friedrich, probably chronological. On the mantel stood two white china candlesticks and a small bronze statuette of Napoleon. In the further corner, to the left of the fireplace, was a high upright cabinet with drawers for manuscripts, prints, etc.; and on the western wall there were bookshelves to right and left of the door leading into the closet behind the partition.

"Against the southern wall stood a low couch with loose leather mattress; while the eastern side, from the corner to the door, was occupied by a long, dwarf, three-tiered bookshelf, the upper half of which was filled with the works of Voltaire, in over ninety volumes. Maps, prints, and engravings, relating almost exclusively to the 'Life of Frederick the Great,' covered the available wall space ; and in one corner stood the long hooked pole by which the balanced frames of the skylight could be opened and closed. Near the fireplace, a little to the left, was the place of the famous writing-table on which so much of noble work had painful birth. The photograph gives so exact an impression of its sturdy frame, its broad folding flap, its slightly boxed top, and back drawers, that no further description is needed either of it or the solid writing-chair. Hard by stood another little table on castors, which carried the books in immediate use (or such as were not on the floor !), while behind was the fourfold screen on which were pasted near a hundred old portrait prints, to which the maker of history always turned for insight and guidance in depicting his characters.

" When Carlyle gave up the use of this room, after the completion of his great history, the pictures, books, and furniture were dispersed elsewhere about the house, and later visitors will remember the writing-desk as standing in the drawing-room, the cabinet of drawers and little table in the dining-room, and many of the prints in the hall, staircase,

MARGARET A CARLYLE

Carlyle's Mother

and elsewhere, as indicated in the Picture List appended."

The 30th of September is given by Professor Norton as the date of Margaret Carlyle's birth, which was evidently unknown to her children when the following letter was written : —

XLV. CARLYLE TO MRS. HANNING, HAMILTON, C. W.

CHELSEA, 8 *April*, 1855.

DEAR SISTER, — I know not if you ever saw our lamented Mother's portrait which was done at Dumfries a good many years ago. It hangs in my room ever since, and has been very sad but precious company to me, as you may fancy, ever since the Christmas day of 1853! I have got seven copies taken of it (done by the machine they call photograph), and this is the one that falls to your share. I can well believe it will be very sad to you, dear little sister, but sacred, too, and very precious. You can easily get it framed in some modest cheap way; it may lie in the cupboard secure from dust till then. The birthday, " 30th Sept.," was not quite certain; Roodfair in the year 1771 was held on the " 25th of Sept.," and whether it was the "Monday after," or the "Monday before" (which would be 23rd Sept.), there was diversity of recollection. I myself and, I think, Jane inclined to think "after;" Jean thought rather the other way: so no date was put upon the Tombstone,—but perhaps you yourself have a better remembrance of what our Mother used to say on that point? Alas, we cannot settle it now, nor is that the important thing we have lost hold of in the change that has happened to us all! But let us not lament; it is far from our part to lament; let us try rather to bless God for having had such a Mother, and to walk always while in this world as she would have wished we might do. Amen, Amen.

There has been nothing wrong since the Doctor's sad loss. Jane and I, in particular, have not been worse than usual, though I think it was the severest winter I ever experienced (certainly far the worst I ever saw here), and has lasted, indeed, almost up to this time — "real spring weather" being yet hardly a week old with us. Sister Jean at Dumfries got a bad whitlow in one of her fingers; and the thrice unlucky blockhead of a Doctor she got there, cut away three

times over some white substance he saw,
which proved to be the sinew (sorrow on
the fool), so that she has now no use of
her (right hand) forefinger, though otherwise
quite recovered again. She has learned to
write with the next finger and makes no complaint.

The Doctor is here for sometime back, and
I think may likely enough continue awhile,
and perhaps draw hither as his main place.
He lodges only about a mile off nearest the
town, so I see him very often — almost every
day in fact. He is very quiet, patiently composed, reads Books, writes letters, runs about;
is chiefly occupied hitherto about his late
wife's affairs, and the three boys (from 12
to 16) whom she left, who are all there staying with him (for a week or two) just now.
Jane is pretty well, for her, and sends her
kind remembrances to "little Jenny." I am
very busy with work, but making hardly any
way in it. Give my best wishes to Robert
and the two little lassies whom I remember
so well. Send me your own address (without
"Gunn," etc., in it) when you write next.
And fare right well, dear sister Jenny.

I am, your affectionate brother,
T. CARLYLE.

In May, 1857, Lady Ashburton died. Both as Lady Harriet Baring and as Lady Ashburton, she had been a friend to Carlyle but a cause of much unhappiness to his wife. Many years after her death Carlyle said of her, " She was the greatest lady of rank I ever saw, with the soul of a princess and captainess had there been any career possible to her but that fashionable one."

Carlyle made a second tour in Germany, in August, 1857, for the purpose of visiting Frederick's battle-fields. In September of the next year the first volumes of the book were published. In December Lord Ashburton married again, and the new Lady Ashburton became a fast friend to both Carlyles.

XLVI. CARLYLE TO MRS. HANNING, HAMILTON, C. W.

CHELSEA, LONDON, 7th *January*, 1859.

DEAR JENNY, — I got your letter acknowledging receipt of the Book; I have more than once got news of you that were welcome since I wrote last, though in general I tried to make some other of our kinsfolk give you notice. Indeed I have been inexpressibly busy for months and for years — with that frightful Book, and other burdens that lay heavy on me. I have in general lived perfectly alone, working all day with what strength remained to so grey a man, then rushing out into the dusk to ride for a couple of hours, then home again to Books, etc. It was seldom that I had leisure to write the smallest note. Indeed, I wrote none except upon compulsion — and never wrote so few in the same length of time on any terms before. I am again busy at the two remaining volumes, almost as busy and miserable as ever, but I cannot go on thinking of you (as you need not doubt I have often enough done) without sometime or other writing, and here has the time at last come by an effort of my own.

You must take this enclosed Paper to some Bank (John says " Any Bank in Canada will do," and " perhaps even give a premium "), the Bank will change it into Canada money (with or without " premium "), and my little Jenny is to accept it as a small New Year's Gift from her Brother. That is all the practical part of this present letter. My blessings conveyed aloud with it, if they could be of any avail, are known to you I hope always without writing.

Your Messenger, a very honest looking

young man, called with the photographs of
the two bairns whom I could hardly recognize, such strapping Iizzies were they grown;
this is a long while since. I carried the
photographs into Annandale with me, where
also they were interesting. Mary at the Gill
now has them, I believe. Give my affectionate remembrances to the originals whom I
always remember as little bairns, though they
are now grown big. May a blessing be on
them, whatever size they grow to; and may
their lot be that of good and honourable
women, useful in their day and generation,
and a credit to those connected with them.
I am very glad to hear what you say of your
household, and judge that you are doing well,
tho' not so rich as some are. A little money
before one's hand is very useful, but much is
not needed. It is written "the hand of the
diligent" does find chances, and "maketh
rich," or rich enough. Give my best wishes
to your Husband — my best encouragements
to persevere in well doing.

The D^r was here a while ago; but he is
off to Annandale again. He has four step-
sons, (children of his late wife,) who form
his main employment in late years and give
him much writing and running about, with

their schooling and affairs. The Austins, it was settled lately, are to stay in the Gill for another seven years, which we were very glad of. Scotsbrig and the other farmers are prosperous — a good time for farmers owing to new railways (I think), and Californian gold, which are resources that will not last for ever. Jean and hers are well. Her eldest son Jamie is, since some months, a clerk in a good mercantile house here and does very well. The Doctor his uncle procured him the place. My Jane has been very weakly for two winters past, but is a little stauncher this winter; a great blessing to us. I sent some books the other day to Alick's Tom; to Alick's self there went a Frederick at the same time as yours, but I have heard yet nothing of it, tho' I persuade myself it, too, is safe. My love to them by the first opportunity. God bless you all.

T. CARLYLE.

XLVII. CARLYLE TO MRS. HANNING, HAMILTON, C. W.

CHELSEA, LONDON, 30 *April*, 1860.

DEAR SISTER JENNY, — I have twice had a Newspaper from you lately, the last time only two days ago; and I am always glad to see such a mark of your remembrance,

and understand by it that things are going
tolerably well with you, or at least not going
far out of course. I would write oftener,
and I hope to do so by and by; but at
present I am kept at such a press as you
have not the least idea of; and, for months
and indeed years past, I have had almost to
cease corresponding with everybody; and
have not, except upon compulsion, written the
smallest Note, — every moment of my time
being so taken up with another dismal kind
of " writing " which I cannot shirk. It is of
no use afflicting you with complaints of what
you cannot help, or with pity for me which
could do no good, but the truth is I never
had in all my life such a frightfully undoable
disgusting piece of work as this which has
been reserved for the *end* of my strength, and
it has made and makes me now and for years
back *miserable* till I see it done. I stick to
it like death and it shall not beat me if I can
help it. No more of it here, — nothing of it,
except to explain my silence; within a couple
of years, if I live so long, I hope to be much
more in case for correspondence with those
whom I merely think of with affection, as
times are.

To-day I have done a little thing which has

been among my purposes for some time, namely, got a small memorial ready for you — which so soon as you have read this note you can go and ask for and so conclude. For the paper of the Messrs. Coutts, Bankers, I conclude, will go in the same steamer as this Note and all will be ripe by the time you have done reading. You are to go to the "Bank of Upper Canada," Hamilton, to say you are "Mrs. Janet Hanning" and that there is £10 for you from "Mr. Thomas Carlyle, London" — upon which they will hand it out and so end. It is a great pleasure to me, dear little Jenny, to think of your getting this poor *fairing* from me, and stitching up for yourself here and there a loose tack with it — as I know you well understand how to do. Do not trouble yourself writing ; address me a newspaper in your own hand and put one stroke on it, that will abundantly tell me whatever is to be said.

Your kindred here and in Scotland are all in their usual course. Nothing wrong with any of them, or nothing to speak of. My own poor Jane has by accident hurt her side a little the other day, which annoys her for the present, but we are promised a "perfect cure in less than four weeks."

The new year took the Carlyles to the Grange again. "Everybody," Carlyle wrote, "as kind as possible, especially the lady. This party small and insignificant; nobody but ourselves and Venables, an honest old dish, and Kingsley, a new, of higher pretensions, but inferior flavour."

Visits in general, however, were rarer than ever in these years of "Frederick," to which every possible moment was devoted. Even Carlyle's letters to his kindred had grown fewer.

XLVIII. CARLYLE TO MRS. HANNING, HAMILTON, C. W.

CHELSEA, LONDON, 28 *Feb'y*, 1861.

DEAR JENNY, — The enclosed bit of paper has lain here for some days back, in the hope that I might find leisure to write you a couple of words along with it. With or without leisure, I had determined to send it to-day, (Friday, which is our American post day), but last night your pleasant little note from Hamilton arrived and that naturally quickened my determination. No man in all the world has less *time* than I, for these many months past and to come, and I write no notes at all unless like this in strictly exceptional cases.

Your account of your laying out the last little New Year's gift is touching and beautiful to me. I know you are a thrifty, gleg creature and wise thrift is becoming much a rarity in our time. The image of your tidy household and of the valiant battle you are fighting far away is worth many pounds to me. If the pinch become sharp at any time, fear not to apply to me. I know you are a proud little soul and somewhat disdain not to do your own turn yourself. All this is right : — nevertheless I expressly tell you (and pray don't neglect it), " send me word when the pinch threatens to be sharp " — which I hope it will not be, only if it is at any time observe what I say and mean here.

We are getting very feckless, Jane and I — partly by advancing years, partly, (in my own case), by such an unutterable quagmire of a job in which I have been labouring for about 10 years — and have still at least one year of it ahead if I live. Want of sleep, I believe, is the latest form of illness with me, latest and most frightful : — but I try to *dodge* it and have still (in secret) a surprising toughness in me for my years. Hope is rising too as the hideous months of a job done at last visibly *diminish*.

All the kindred in Scotland are well —
under date three or four days ago. The Dr.
is spending this winter in Edinburgh : — has
still no hearth of his own but lives in lodgings, shifting about. Jean and her affairs
are prosperous, thinking of " buying a house"
&c. Jamie, her oldest boy, is a very douce,
well-doing clerk in the City here for two
years past or more. Young Jamie of Scotsbrig, owing to health, had to give up that
and is now with his father thinking to be a
farmer. Times are good with them at Scotsbrig, though our poor brother Jamie is in
weak health and silently feels his " hervist
endit." Poor fellow ! still I send my good
wishes heartily to your good Robert. I am
always, dear little Jenny,

Your truly affectionate,
T. Carlyle.

In April, 1861, Carlyle went to hear Ruskin's lecture on " Leaves;" and in August,
1862, highly praised to Erskine the same
writer's " Unto this Last."

April 29, 1863, Carlyle wrote thus of one
of Dickens's readings: " I had to go yesterday
to Dickens's Reading, 8 p. m. Hanover Rooms,
to the complete upsetting of my evening habi-

tudes and spiritual composure.   Dickens does
do it capitally, such as *it* is ; acts better than
any Macready in the world; a whole tragic,
comic, heroic *theatre* visible, performing under
one *hat*, and keeping us laughing — in a sorry
way, some of us thought — the whole night.
He is a good creature, too, and makes fifty or
sixty pounds by each of these readings."

Carlyle's unfortunate horse, mentioned in
the following letter, was Fritz.   He was sold
for nine pounds.   Lady Ashburton supplied
a successor, whom Carlyle called Noggs.

XLIX. CARLYLE TO MRS. HANNING, HAMILTON, C. W.

CHELSEA, LONDON, 13 *Aug.* 1863.

DEAR SISTER JENNY, — It is a long time
since I have had on hand to send you the
little bit of remembrance marked on the other
page, but I am held in such a ferment of perpetual hurry and botheration here and have
grown so weak and weary of my sad work,
(till it *do* end), that I have seldom five minutes
to dispose of in my own way, and leave many
little jobs undone for a long time and many
little satisfactions unenjoyed for want of a bold
stroke at them.   Finally I bethought me of
the Dr. in Edinburgh and he has now got me
your little paper into readiness for sending.

I understand you have nothing to do but present it at the Bank and at once get payment. If, (till you have time to write a long letter of *news*, which will be very welcome), you at once address me a Canada newspaper with three strokes, nothing more will be necessary in regard to this little bit of business.

I expect to get done with my book in six or eight months. O that I saw the day! I can and have been working thitherward with all the strength that I possess, to the hurt of my health as well, but I calculate when the end have once come I shall begin directly to improve more or less, and perhaps by degrees get very considerably better again. I had an excellent horse who had carried me 7 years and above twenty thousand miles, his hoofs were got spoiled on the stone hard roads. He came plunging down with me one day, (not throwing me nor hurting me in the slightest), —a most decided fall for no reason whatever—upon which I had to sell him (to a kind master for an old song), and for the last six weeks have been *walking*, which was a great enjoyment by way of change. It would not do, however, and since about a week I am mounted again : — very swift, very rough (in comparison to my old friend), but good

natured, healthy, willing : — and must continue adding a dozen miles daily to the twenty
thousand already done.

We have had such a winter for *warmth* as
was never seen before, not very healthy, I believe, but it has agreed well with Jane : — and
indeed the kindred, I think, are all well. Poor
" Wullie Carlyle " (if you remember him at
all) died lately at Edinburgh, an old man, as
we are all growing hereabouts.

Tell Alick about my affairs and this last
news you have had. That I never do or can
forget him, he need not be told. I hope your
lasses are doing well and that Robert and all
of you are pushing along patiently, faithfully
as heretofore.

In August, 1863, Mrs. Carlyle fell in St.
Martin's Lane and broke her thigh. The
accident resulted in long illness and pain.
During the spring of 1864 she grew worse,
and in March was taken to St. Leonards.
From a subsequent trip to Scotland she returned in October to Cheyne Row, " weak,
shattered, body worn to a shadow, spirit bright
as ever."

The last volume of " Frederick " was published in April, 1865. When the proofs were

finished, Carlyle and his wife went to Devon-
shire for a few weeks with Lady Ashburton.

CHELSEA, 4 *May*, 1865.

DEAR JENNY, — Two or three days ago, I
saw a letter from you to Sister Jean; which
was very welcome here, as bringing more defi-
nite news of you than we had got for a good
while before. I have now got done with my
Book (a copy of it probably in your hands
before this); and am not henceforth to be so
dreadfully hampered in writing a little note to
my friends from time to time. I am still in a
huge fuss, confusions of all kinds lying about
me, and indeed I am just about running off
for Scotland (to Jean's, in the first place), to
try and recover a little from the completely
shattered state these twelve years of incessant
drudgery and slaving have reduced me to.
But there is something I had meant, this long
time and here it is — just come to hand. In-
closed is a Paper which will bring you the
amount of Dollars for £20, on your presenting it at the Hamilton Bank. If by way of
"*identifying,*" they ask you who *sends* the
money, you can answer with my name, and if
further needful, add that the Negotiator for

me with the Edinr. Bank, was *Dr.* Carlyle of that City. Nothing more, I suppose, if even that much will be necessary. Let me know by return that it is safe in your hand (a newspaper with *three* strokes will serve if you are short of time for the moment). And so with my best blessings, dear little Jenny, accept this poor mark of my remembrance.

My Jane is very frail and feeble, but always stirring about, and has got blessedly away out of the horrible torments she had (and all of you had on her account) last year. Scotsbrig, Gill, Dumfries, Edinburgh; all is going in the usual average way there. To you I can fancy what a distress the removal of your poor little Mary and her Husband to the Far West must be! These things happen and are *inevitable* in the current of life. That your son-in-law is a good man, this should be a great joy to you. Do not you be *too* hasty to follow to Iowa; consider it well first.

You see what a shaky hand I have; you do not see the bitter hurry I am still in! With kindest wishes to you and all your household,

Ever your Affectionate Brother,

T. CARLYLE.

Carlyle was elected Lord Rector of the University of Edinburgh in November, 1865; and on April 2, 1866, spoke his inaugural address at Edinburgh, of which the best account known to me — best for a general impression of Carlyle — is that given by Mr. Moncure Conway. On the 21st of April the news of Mrs. Carlyle's sudden death was brought to Carlyle at his sister's house in Dumfries. The epitaph which he wrote for her grave in the abbey church of Haddington ends with the words, " And the light of his life as if gone out."

An episode of the time when that light was fading will remain longer with some of us than most of the occurrences of Carlyle's life. Mrs. Oliphant has left a sketch, done with very few lines, of Mrs. Carlyle playing Scotch airs " to the tall old man in his dressing-gown, sitting meditative by the fire." Carlyle himself, in his Journal for December 3, 1867, described the last of these occasions: " One evening, I think in the spring of 1866, we two had come up from dinner and were sitting in this room, very weak and weary creatures, perhaps even I the wearier, though she far the weaker; I at least far the more inclined to sleep, which directly after dinner was not good for me. ' Lie on the sofa there,' said she — the ever

kind and graceful, herself refusing to do so—
'there, but don't sleep,' and I, after some
superficial objecting, did.   In old years I used
to lie that way, and she would play the piano
to me: a long series of Scotch tunes which set
my mind finely wandering through the realms
of memory and romance, and effectually pre-
vented sleep.   That evening I had lain but a
few minutes when she turned round to her
piano, got out the Thomson Burns book, and,
to my surprise and joy, broke out again into
her bright little stream of harmony and poesy,
silent for at least ten years before, and gave
me, in soft tinkling beauty, pathos, and melody,
all my old favourites: 'Banks and Braes,'
'Flowers of the Forest,' 'Gilderoy,' not for-
getting 'Duncan Gray,' 'Cauld Kail,' 'Irish
Coolen,' or any of my favourites tragic or comic.
. . . That piano has never again sounded, nor
in my time will or shall.   In late months it
has grown clearer to me than ever that she
had said to herself that night, 'I will play his
tunes all yet once,' and had thought it would
be but once. . . . This is now a thing infi-
nitely touching to me.   So like her; so like
her.   Alas, alas!   I was very blind, and might
have known better how near its setting my
bright sun was."

The following letter is shadowed with the death of Mrs. Carlyle, although nearly two years had passed.

LI. CARLYLE TO MRS. HANNING, HAMILTON, C. W.

CHELSEA, 14*th February*, 1868.

MY DEAR JENNY, — This is a little New Year's gift which I intended for you sooner. It (the essential part of it) has been lying here apart and wrapt up for you ever since Christmas time, but I never could get up to have it made into a banking, portable form till now, so languid, sad and lazy have I been! The banks all close at an earlier hour than my walking one, and it is rare that I can get so far into town in time. I am dreadfully indisposed to writing, and even my poor shaking right hand makes continual protest! I hope the poor little Gift will be welcome to you and in some savings bank or otherwise be innocently waiting to do you good some time or other! — I am told there will be no difficulty for you at the " Gore Bank " in Hamilton merely to go thither and sign your name. A newspaper with three strokes will sufficiently announce it for me till you have leisure for writing. I have also sent a photograph for nephew Tom's young wife, to whom, with all

THOMAS CARLYLE

my affectionate regards to them both, pray
send it by your first opportunity. There is
another (if the letter will carry it), for yourself for your own free disposal otherwise.

I am not specially in worse health than
usual, but excessively languid, dispirited,
weary, sad and idle — especially in the late
dark months of winter, which however are
now gone, and indeed were never severe but
lighter upon us than common. Jean has
been here ever since early in December. It
makes the house a little less lonesome to me
than it has become for the last twenty two
months, but cannot, as you may imagine, lift
the heavy heart of me into anything of
cheeriness, nor indeed perhaps *should* it.
She will go home by Liverpool before long,
where her son Jim (who is a clever solid fellow and has got promotion in Liverpool) is
just setting up house with his sister Maggie
as Manageress. Their mother will look in so
soon as they have the home settled. All
kinds of business are reported as utterly *dull*
here; much distress among the idle poor —
and a general silent anxiety as to this new
" Reform Bill " or " Leap in the dark," —
poor stupid souls !

An extremely accursed atrocity of murder

and worse has happened in Cummertrees,
which has thrown all the community into
horror and excitation — of which you will
see or hear soon enough in the newspapers
and probably know the location as I do.
Your kindred in Annandale and here are all
well and I can send their best regards.

Ever your affectionate brother,

T. CARLYLE.

In October, 1868, Carlyle was again thrown,
— this time from a horse named Comet.   A
conversation with the Queen, the death of
Mr. Erskine of Linlathen, and a letter to
the Times newspaper on the Franco-Prussian
war were among the events of the next few
years.

Carlyle speaks again now of his shaking
right hand.   A few weeks after he quite lost
the use of it for writing with a pen.   " Mary
Aitken," ready to write to his dictation, was
Mary Carlyle Aitken, daughter to his sister
Jean.

LII.   CARLYLE TO MRS. HANNING, HAMILTON, C. W.

5 Cheyne Row, Chelsea, 13 *Feb.* 1871.

My dear Sister Jenny, — Here is a little
bit of a present which you must accept from

me ; it was intended for the New Year's time, but has been belated ; which will do it no great ill with you. Buy yourself something nice with it ; and consider at all times that my affectionate best wishes are with you ; and that if I could in any way do you a useful kindness, I gladly would.

We get a good few Canada newspapers from you ; welcome tokens of your remembrance : in one of the last, there was a very melancholy item of news marked by your hand, — the death of your dear little grandchild, poor Mary's Bairn ; we conceived painfully how sad it must have made you all ; and were ourselves sad and sorry. Poor Mary, she was herself a child when I saw her last, and she is now a bereaved mother : — Death snatches us from one another at all ages! I often think with silent gratitude to Providence how gently we older ones have been dealt with in this respect ; saved, a whole family of us, for so many years ; none lost but poor Margaret, (very dear, and very sacred to me at this hour), and a wee wee *Jenny* whom you never saw, but whose death, and my mother's unappeasable grief for it, are still strangely present to me, after near seventy years. All we can say is, both the

Living and the Dead are with God; and we have to obey, and be of hope.

You regret sometimes that I do not write to you; but it is not my blame, it is my misfortune rather. For rather above five years past my right hand has been getting useless for writing, (the left strangely enough, is still steady, and holds good); the weight of years, too, 75 of them gone December last, presses heavy on me; and all work, but most especially all kinds of writing, are a thing I avoid as sorrowfully disagreeable. Mary Aitken, who drives an admirable pen, is indeed ever willing to be "dictated" to; and I do, in cases of necessity, trust that method; but find, on the whole, that it never will succeed with me.

From the Dr. and from Jean I believe you get all the news that are worth writing; and that is the main interest in the matter.

The Dr. is in Edinburgh of late weeks, and seems to be enjoying himself among old friends: — and finds it, no doubt, a pleasant and useful interruption of his Dumfries solitude, to which he will return with fresh appetite. He is much stronger and cheerier than I; five years *younger*, and at least twice five lighter of heart. He has an excellent lodging

at Dumfries yonder; and is of much service
to all the kindred; every one of whom he is
continally ready to help. Mary Aitken has
been here with me above two years: — a
bright little soul, writing for me, trying to be
useful and cheerful to me. I have plenty of
friends here; but none of them do me much
good, except by their evident good-will; company in general is at once wearisome and
hurtful to me; silence, and the company of
my own sombre thoughts, sad probably, but
also loving and beautiful, are wholesomer
than talking; these and a little serious reading are my chief resource. I have no bodily
ailment, except what belongs to the grad-
ual decay of a digestive faculty which was
always weak; except when sleepless nights
afflict me too much, I have no reason to com-
plain, but the contrary. This winter, now
nearly done, has been a blusterous, cold, inclement one as any I can latterly remember;
it grew at last to tell upon me as the un-
friendliest of all its brethren: — but I think,
after all, it may have done me little or no
intrinsic damage. With the new Spring and
its bright days I hope to awaken again and
shake away this torpor of nerves and mind.
I have long owed Alick a letter — that is to

say, intended to write him one, though by
count it is his turn. I often think of you
all on that side the Sea as well as this; if
that could do you any good. Alas! I will
end here, dear little Sister; wishing all that
is good to you and yours, as at all times. I
am and remain,

> Ever your affectionate Brother,
> > T. CARLYLE.

Send a *newspaper* with 3 strokes when
this comes: don't trouble yrself with any
other announcement.

In November, 1872, Emerson made his
last visit to England. Carlyle was now reduced to writing " in largish letters with blue
pencil." After the next letter he never wrote
again with his own hand to Mrs. Hanning
or to any member of the family across the
Atlantic.

LIII. CARLYLE TO MRS. HANNING, HAMILTON, C. W.

> CHELSEA, 2 *Jan*ʸ 1873.

DEAR SISTER JENNY, — I please myself
with the thought that you will accept this little Newyear's Gift from me as a sign of my
unalterable affection, whᵇ tho' it is obliged

to be silent (unable to *write* as of old) cannot fade away until I myself do! Of that be always sure, my dear little sister, — and that if in anything I can be of help to you or yours, I right willingly will.

"Clinthill's" Photograph is wonderful and deeply affecting to me. Not one feature in it can I recognize as his: such are the changes half-a-century works upon us! If you have any means, send him my affectionate remembrances and unchanged good-wishes.

No more from this lame hand, dear sister Jenny, — except my heart's blessings for the year and forever.

Y.^r affect.^e Brother,
T. CARLYLE.

LIV. MISS MARY CARLYLE AITKEN TO MRS. HANNING, HAMILTON, C. W.

5 CHEYNE ROW, CHELSEA,
3 *Feb.* 1874.

MY DEAR AUNT, — Your little note arrived duly and was very welcome; telling as it did that all was well with you in your far off home. I have several times lately intended to write to you, spontaneously, but somehow one's time seems to get so filled up that few of all the things one proposes to do get

accomplished. I was very glad of the little
note which you sent sometime ago in answer
to one from me, and would have taken up
Cousin Kate's Challenge as to writing, but
had a great deal of writing to do at that time
and was moreover in very indifferent health,
— or I certainly should have written to her.
I hope she is getting on well. We had a
very good account of her from Alick and
James Carlyle when they were here.

Uncle has been pretty well all the winter,
until a fortnight ago, when he caught cold,
which has troubled him a good deal; but he
is getting rid of it now. Last August he
and I went to Norfolk, and, after spending
ten days very pleasantly there, during which
time he seemed every day to grow younger
and better, we turned our faces to the north.
After a disagreeable journey to Newcastle by
steamer, went on to Dumfries, where we found
everybody well; from Dumfries we made several excursions, — to the Gill, where all were
prospering, and especially Jane, who used to
look rather thin and delicate, was looking
very well. Aunt Mary is one of the kindest
people one ever sees; she looked older than
she did when I saw her before; and is generally rather serious than lively. They have

got on their farm for another nineteen years at a very small increase of rent, which must be a great comfort to them. We one day went to Scotsbrig, where I have not been more than about three times in my life. John's wife, whom I never saw before, looks very amiable and gentle, rather than clever and smart; they have three children, one boy and two girls, one of the latter about the prettiest little thing I ever saw. Uncle Jamie had unfortunately made a mistake as to the day of our coming; so that we did not see him then; but he came to Dumfries and was looking very well; though, poor man, he has had a hard enough time of it since; for his daughter Jenny has been very ill all the winter; as it was she lost her little daughter; and last Sunday night poor Jenny's long, painful illness ended in death. I think she has left three children. It must be a cruel blow to Uncle Jamie, who always seemed so fond of her. We have been expecting no other news than this for some time back; but when death comes it never fails to surprize. There have been a great many deaths amongst us the last year or two; you are well off, dear Aunt, to have all your children spared to you. My Mother when I saw her

in Summer did not seem to have forgotten
those that were taken away. We used to be
very fond of singing songs together in the
evenings, but when we once tried it last time
I was at home, one after another of us broke
down until we had to give up the one solitary
attempt. At Ecclefechan I went with the
two Uncles to see the houses in which they
were born and also to see Grandfather's and
Grandmother's graves. I don't remember
ever to have seen Ecclefechan before. It was
a very interesting day we spent; none of us
were in high spirits, as you may suppose; but
it is very pleasant to me to look back upon
the visit. Uncle and I went also to Fife to
visit the Welsh's (Aunt Jane's Cousins) and
after two or three days there we spent a day
at Haddington; staid one night in Edinburgh and, after seeing one or two people
there, returned to Dumfries, and after a week
or two to Chelsea, — having been away in all
only about six weeks. Uncle was not very
well and complained of the noise of the railway whistle &c. at Dumfries; and so we
were not sorry to be back to Chelsea again;
I am hoping to get away for a week or
two this spring to see them all at home, if
Miss Welsh comes on a visit, as she may very

possibly do. Uncle has not been working at anything lately; he spends nearly all his time in reading. I am very glad to be back with him again, although I was sorry to leave the Taylors, who are very good people, and were most kind to me. I got on there very well, only I was in bad health nearly all the time. However, I am very much better now.

I have written this note, or rather long scrawl, in great haste; and have been often interrupted, so I hope you will excuse it — as, if I read it over, I shall be sure not to send it off and have not time at present to write another. Uncle sends his kindest love and best wishes, as well as thanks for your kind letter, with all good messages from myself.

Ever, dear Aunt,
Your affectionate
MARY CARLYLE AITKEN.

During the month in which the last letter was written, Carlyle received the Prussian Order of Merit, and, later in the year, refused the Grand Cross of the Bath, offered by Disraeli.

"Bield" was the name of Alexander Carlyle's farm.

LV. CARLYLE TO MRS. HANNING. HAMILTON, C. W.

5 Cheyne Row, Chelsea,
12 April, 1875.

My dear Sister Jenny, — It is a long
time since I have heard direct from you; and
a good deal longer since I wrote myself.
But we see all your letters to the Dr., yours
and your children's; and I hope and indeed
even know, that you never doubt of my brotherly remembrance and affectionate thoughts
of you all. Silent my thoughts are obliged
mostly to be, for my hand this long while
back is quite useless for writing and indeed
even by dictation I never do write except on
absolute compulsion. This time I send you a
small practical memorial of which you will
see the nature from Adamson the Banker's
little note enclosed; which I hope you will
have no difficulty in negotiating and turning
into dollars. Pray accept it kindly, and lay
it out in buying yourself any little thing you
find useful or agreeable to you, — or lay it
by if you like better, added to any little *pose*
of your own against a rainy day. Do not
trouble yourself with writing any answer;
merely send me an old newspaper, addressed
in your own hand with three strokes, which

will be taken as a sure sign that you have got it all right.

I have grown very old (now getting fast forward with my 80th year) and am very weak and useless, as is natural; but by blessing from above, still wonderfully keep my health, what health I could expect to have; and have suffered little or nothing by the late severe winter, which also I find has been so severe with you. Take care of yourself in the bitter cold when it comes again; and above all provide yourself with effectual warm clothing. I read with interest your daughter Mary's letter: and was glad after all that you had been so kind as to go to Bield on report of Billy Bobby, tho' the reception there was not quite of the kind one could have wished. Alas, alas! Perversity is born with us all, and comes out in little touches, where we least expected it. The one remedy is to crush it down each of us for himself, and in respect of others to forgive and forget. Our spring here is very tardy; the weather still damp, chill and disagreeable. I hope it may be much brighter with you, thanks to your deep, clear skies; not drowned in mist like ours, and that it may be shining summer when this arrives. This morning we

had a letter from the Dr. who reports all the
kindred well.   He proposes to come up hither
about the end of the month; he has been
much more quiescent this season than I have
often known him; but is about to move at
last.   God bless you always, dear Jenny, you
and yours.

    I am and remain

        Ever your affectionate Brother

                T. CARLYLE.

Carlyle's eightieth birthday — December 4,
1875 (year of " Early Kings of Norway " and
" Portraits of John Knox ") — was celebrated
with a memorial from his friends and "a whirl-
wind of gifts and congratulations."   In February, 1876, John Forster died, and in April
Carlyle's brother Alexander.   Carlyle wrote
in his Journal: " Young Alick's account of
his death is altogether interesting — a scene
of sublime simplicity, great and solemn under
the humblest forms.   That question of his,
when his eyes were already shut, and his
mind wavering before the last *finis* of all: —
' Is Tom coming from Edinburgh the Morn?'
will never leave me should I live a hundred years.   Poor Alick, my ever faithful brother! Come back across wide oceans and long

decades of time to the scenes of brotherly companionship with me, and going out of the world as it were with his hand in mine. Many times he convoyed me to meet the Dumfries coach, or to bring me home from it, and full of bright and perfect affection always were those meetings and partings."

The last bit of Carlyle's writing printed during his life was a letter to the " Times," in May, 1877, on the Russo-Turkish war. In the same year Boehm made a statue of Carlyle, and Millais a portrait.

" 24 Cheyne Row " was the new (and present) numbering of Carlyle's house.

LVI. CARLYLE TO DR. JOHN CARLYLE, DUMFRIES.

24 Cheyne Row, Chelsea,
21 Sep. 1878.

MY DEAR BROTHER, — We got your letter this morning, and were very glad to hear that things went so tolerably with you in your present sad imprisonment. We had not the bit of bad weather you speak of, or had it only in a milder type. We also get out daily in a drive of two hours which might be pleasanter were we in better circumstances to enjoy it, but it does us good and forms a

variety in our rather stagnant ways. I also
contrive to get some modicum of sleep every
night and have now got rested from the great
confusions of our journey hither, in which till
Crewe we could get no place to ourselves.
The scene on Carlisle platform was beyond
all others I have seen the most chaotic and
disturbing to me. The Town seems quite
empty of people we have business with. We
have seen only Blakiston and his Bessy Blakiston is as nonsensical as formerly. He spoke
of writing to you, but I know not whether he
has done it. His knowledge about your circumstances seems to me to amount to zero.
Yesterday we called at Darwin's door, heard
he was in his usual way of health, but as
nephews of his had just driven up to his door,
we did not venture in. Froude is still at
Saltcombe for a month to come. Till then
does not make his appearance here. I have
nearly done my reperusal of *Frederick* and
know not what book next to apply to. But
something I will devise for that poor purpose.
The Town is very empty, but begins in a slow
way to repeople itself.

We are much concerned to hear by James
of Newlands that poor Austin lies at the Gill
in dangerous circumstances; jaundice is the

last figure of his illness. May, it appears, is
in her usual way. Here our weather is generally good and I often have a walk down to
the bottom of the embankment, which is
strange and I suppose salutary to me. A sad
thought to me in this operation is that, alas,
you cannot share it with me, or for the present enjoy anything like it. No word from
Canada, but certainly some must be coming.
My kindest love to Jean. Tell her if I had
a *hand*, she should not long expect a letter
from me! With kindest love to one and all
of you,

    I ever am

        Your affecte Brother,

            T. CARLYLE.

Will you kindly send *Emerson* back when
everybody has done with it.

John Carlyle died in 1879. Carlyle was
now growing steadily weaker, and by October
of 1880 was under the constant care of a physician.

Mary Aitken, by marriage with her cousin
Alexander Carlyle, was now become "Mary
Carlyle."

LVII. MRS. ALEXANDER CARLYLE TO MRS. HANNING,
HAMILTON, C. W.

24 Cheyne Row, Chelsea,
18 *July*, 1880.

My dear Aunt, — I received my Cousin
Mrs. Baird's letter about ten days ago, asking
for tidings of my Uncle. I am extremely
sorry that you have been made anxious about
him through my not writing; but indeed
there have been many sufficient apologies
for my want of punctuality in that way,
which, however, I need not trouble you with
here. It will suffice to say that I use the
very first chance I have had to answer your
enquiries.

It is not very easy to explain to you exactly
how Uncle is. He is exceedingly weak,
hardly able to walk fifty yards without help,
and yet until about ten days ago, when he
had a very severe attack of Diarrhœa which
has left him much below *par*, he was what
one might call for him very well. He generally spends his mornings till about half past
two o'clock between lying on the sofa, reading in his easy chair, and smoking an occa-
sional pipe; at half past two he goes out to
drive for two or two and a half hours, sleeps

JANET CARLYLE HANNING

At the age of 82

on the sofa till dinner time (half past six)
then after dinner sleeps again, at nine has
tea, reads or smokes or talks, or lies on the
sofa till bed time, which is usually about midnight, and so ends the day. He looks very
well in the face, has a fine, fresh ruddy complexion and an immense quantity of white
hair, his voice is clear and strong, he sees and
hears quite well; but for the rest, as I have
said, he is not good at moving about. In
general he is wonderfully good humored and
contented; and on the whole carries his
eighty-four years well. He desires me to
send you his kind love, and his good wishes:
as you know, he writes to nobody at all. I
do not think he has written a single letter,
even dictated one, for over a year.

We are very glad to hear that all is well
with you and with all your family. I have
not time for more just now, as I am interrupted. Good-bye, dear aunt.

I am, Your affectionate Niece,

MARY CARLYLE.

Carlyle died on the 5th of February, 1881.
The Abbey was offered, but refused; and,
as the world knows, Carlyle was buried in
the kirkyard of his native Ecclefechan. The

following narrative of the funeral is from the pen of Mr. John Carlyle Aitken, brother to Mary Aitken Carlyle.

One likes his letters less than his sister's, which are perfect in their unaffected plainness.

The three remaining letters need neither explanation nor comment.

LVIII. MR. JOHN CARLYLE AITKEN TO MRS. HANNING, HAMILTON, C. W.

THE HILL, DUMFRIES, N. B.
11 *Feb.*, 1881.

MY DEAR AUNT, — Today I mean only to write a note of the more needful details, reserving for a more fitting time the full statement. I need not worry you with the account of my tempestuous voyage from New York, in which I made acquaintance with a hurricane, and its full meaning — nor how glad I was at sight of the dear *bare* and rugged hills of my native land — Leaving America to the Americans — and welcome! I shall think for sometime ere I do the " herring-pond" again! Well, no more of that if you love me! no more o' that! I am home, and well, and likely to remain there for the remainder of my days in one shape or other. Let that serve just now on that score.

You would observe the date of Uncle's death and might hear of it the same day, as I thought. At all events The Scotsman would supply more details; and that I hope reached you all right. All has been in such hurry, bustle and confusion ever since that no one has had time to think of writing anything requiring time or calm consideration. Uncle had not been considered seriously ill more than about a fortnight or so before the end. The vital spark of life towards the last days kept flickering in a way so extraordinary that the Doctor declared he had never met such tenacity of life and vitality in the whole course of his varied London and other experience. Dear Uncle, the good, true and noble old man that he was, really suffered little in the way of pain for some weeks before his death, which was itself little more than a gentle flickering sleep, ending in a scarcely heard last sigh of sound. While lying in a comatose or unconscious state his mind seemed to wander back to old Annandale memories of his ever loved ones and their surroundings; his mother holding her supreme seat surrounded by a trooping throng of once familiar faces, not very greatly less dear to him. He died full of years, with all his weary task of world's work well and nobly done, and leaves no mortal behind him who does not love and reverence his life and memory.

By the newspapers I send today you may see how very quiet the funeral yesterday was. The vale of Annan was grim and wintry. You could catch a glimpse of Hoddam, the Brownmuir, Woodcockaigne, and all the old places through the white roupy mist hanging over and round them. The most touching sight I saw was that of three gray haired, smooth crowned fathers of the village of Ecclefechan, who stood together by the wayside, bare-headed and with unfeigned sadness of face and manner silently and impressively bearing witness to their sorrow. It was really very touching to look upon. The Presbyterian Kirk bells tolled mournfully as they laid him gently in the bed of rest within a few yards of the place where he first drew the breath of life, and all was as unostentatious as he himself desired it might be. Ah, me! Ah, me! Uncle James was there, as the last male link of the ever shortening chain. Mother bids me send her love to you and your fellow mourners who here and over all the wide world are many. All would gladly unite in sympathy and love with you in your far away home.

Ever affectionately,
JOHN C. AITKEN.

LIX. MRS. ALEXANDER CARLYLE TO MRS. HANNING, HAMILTON, C. W.

24 CHEYNE ROW, CHELSEA,
3 March, 1881.

MY DEAR AUNT,—Alick received two kind notes from you and Kate, which I will answer as well as I can. The news itself you would receive almost too soon! When we were at Dumfries (where we stayed from Thursday till Monday) John wrote to you and told you some particulars, no doubt more will be welcome, and it would have been natural we should have written ere this, but there has been little composure to write to anyone, and a very great many letters coming every day to be attended to in one shape or another. Last July, as I think I told you, Uncle had a short though rather bad turn of illness evidently brought on by the heat; he seemed to a great extent to recover from it, but he never got up any considerable strength after it; he seemed to grow a little weaker month by month and week by week. He was out on New Year's Day for the last time, a short drive of an hour or so; he complained of the fatigue very much after he came back. He was confined to his bed exactly three weeks all but a day. Until the last few days he was, though now and then delirious, for the most part quiet and collected, and able to talk to us, which he did with great kindness and affection. For the last two days and nights he was in a deep unnatural looking sleep, and except once when he seemed to be trying to speak to us, and he said distinctly " Alick " — and " Woman," he hardly once looked up or moved. On Saturday morning about eight (Alick and I having both sat up with him) I was in the room alone, and at 8.30 I noticed a change in the breathing, at first it seemed to stop, then there were one or two louder breaths and all was over. In the last few days his mind seemed to turn altogether to the old Ecclefechan days; he often took Alick for his Father (Uncle Sandy) and he would put his arms round my neck and say to me, " My dear Mother." His was a great and noble life. I have no words to tell how much I miss him and how sad I feel now that he is gone. I am sure you would get a great

shock when you heard of it. We have formed
no plans yet for the future, but we mean to
keep together all the furniture and Books in
memory of him as long as we live and not to
sell any part of them.

In Scotland we found them all pretty well.
John [her brother] was there as you know,
looking no worse for his multifarious adventures in America. He spoke enthusiastically
of your kindness to him for which we are all
most grateful to you. They then spoke of
writing to you very shortly. Alick and I
drove to the Gill one afternoon and found
them all pretty well there. Aunt Mary,
though complaining of a bad cold, looked as
well as when I saw her before. The other
branches of the family were well, but as we
had so little time I did not see any of them.
I went with the funeral to the gate of the
Kirkyard at poor old Ecclefechan; but I kept
behind the curtain in the carriage, and saw,
or was seen by nobody. I hope to send you
some little memorial of him and I will not forget Kate's request for some little thing of the
kind. I hope all is well with you and yours,
dear Aunt, and that you will excuse me if I
have failed to tell you anything that would be
interesting to you. Give Alick's thanks and

his and my kind regards to Kate, and with
many kind regards to you all,

    I am,

        Ever your affectionate Niece,
            MARY CARLYLE.

An anonymous writer sent to the Pall Mall
Gazette in 1885 a record of travel in Dum-
friesshire, with the title Carlyle's Country.
A selection from it follows:—

"The next point in my pilgrimage was
Mainhill, a farmhouse about two miles from
the village of Ecclefechan. Here, again, I
fancy Mr. Froude gives a rather erroneous
impression. The situation is not very bleak
or cheerless, nor very high; but perhaps he
may have judged of it by the day he visited
the place — on the day when Carlyle was
buried. I was told — my informant being no
other than the man who had tolled the bell
for the funeral — that it was a 'clarty day:'
and as the term was to me technical, I had it
amplified: 'It blawed, it snawed, an' it rained,
an' sleeted. O, it was verra clarty!'

"On such a day I can well understand that
Mainhill would be dreary enough. It was
damp and wet the day I was there, and I carried away from the farm road dust, in the shape

of mud ankle deep, that refused to be shaken
off. The house must have been small indeed
for such a family as the Carlyles: only three
rooms of any kind for all purposes, no 'upper
ben' at all: apparently the sleeping accom-
modation was arranged as on shipboard, by
berths one above the other. It was at Mainhill that Carlyle spent his vacations during his
schoolmaster's and tutorship period: the most
miserable and unhappy period of his whole life.
Wandering upon the hills above Mainhill he
meditated on his unsuccessful efforts at getting
under way, and had it not been for the kindly
and tolerant refuge he here found, he might
well have ended in despair all his valorous
attempts to 'open his oyster:' as it was, he
says, 'almost had I desisted, as obstinately did
it continue shut.' When the early romance
of his first love was rudely ended, these hills
witnessed the weary and hopeless journeyings
which are magnified into the world-wide
wanderings of the sorrows of Teufelsdröckh.
Here he heard pealing in his ears the everlasting No, and sank into the centre of indiffer-
ence, and finally emerged into the calmness of
the everlasting Yea. I purposed, with these
thoughts as comrades, a walk over these same
hills, Burnswark and its neighboring heights

— but alas! the heavenly powers forbade, the landscape was blotted out by foul mists, and the drenching rain descended and effectually drove me back. Gladly did I take refuge in the railway station, and more gladly, though stiff with cold and weariness, did I enter the kindly hostelry at Dumfries, where I ate the repast of the hungry, and slept the sleep of the laboring man, which is sweet, whether he eat little or much."

After describing Craigenputtock, the writer in the Pall Mall Gazette continues: —

" It struck me as a little strange that in a house so associated with Carlyle, given by him to his own university, there should be no mark or token of the connection. Surely the university might make some little acknowledgment to the memory of the donor in the house he had given. If there were a good engraving of him, or a copy of his works — some memento, however slight — it would appear more gracious. But the stranger might come and go away and never know that Craigenputtock was bequeathed to the University of Edinburgh by Thomas Carlyle. I next retraced my way over the moor and down to the valley. I changed my route here, wishing to see Auldgarth Bridge, and to go by Templand to Thornhill, and thence to Annan once more. Auldgarth is hardly more than a mile from Ellesland, and again it seemed hard to tear one's self from Burns, but I had not leisure for both. From Thornhill the steam engine whirls me back to Dumfries and on to Annan once more. I had only one more spot to visit, Scotsbrig, near Ecclefechan, and I could spare no more than another day : by taking an early train from Annan to Kirtlebridge and thence walking by Birrens and Middlebie, I could accomplish my purpose. It was still early — before nine o'clock — when I reached the farm house of Scotsbrig, the house of Carlyle's parents after their removal from Mainhill, and then of his youngest brother James till a few years ago. My reception here was anything but hospitable. I felt myself looked upon with suspicion as some kind of a tramp, and to none of my questions could I get more than a monosyllabic answer. The morning was raw and damp and ungenial, a drizzling rain was falling, and I soon left Scotsbrig, with no very pleasant recollections. The farm house is prettily situated on a little bluff overhanging the burn, which tumbles over the rocks in a pretty little cascade just below the house. A

tramp through the muddy roads brought me
again to the railway, and my pilgrimage was
over."

LX. MR. JOHN CARLYLE AITKEN TO MRS. HANNING,
HAMILTON, C. W.

THE HILL, DUMFRIES, N. B., 11 May, 1890.

MY DEAR AUNT, — Although long ere this
reaches you, you will have heard the sad
news of the death of Uncle James of Scotsbrig, at John Carlyle, his son's farm, of Pingle,
some ten miles nearer the English Border
than Ecclefechan, on Sunday morning the
fourth of May at two o'clock.

I know that you may like to hear anything
in the shape of details. We were all very
sad to think that the last brother was gone,
although in the course of human things otherwise the time could not have been greatly
extended. He had been pretty well confined
to the house and to his bed for seven weeks
or so before, and John C. seemed to say
that the end was rather painful, on account
of his sufferings which no human aid could
materially alleviate, than unexpected in any
way. The funeral was at Ecclefechan on
Wednesday the seventh, or that is to say,
some three days after his death. And I was

the only nephew present and the others were
grandsons, two of Craigenputtock and three
of John's own sons, all nice lads. The train
started from Pingle at eleven, coming to
Ecclefechan by way of Waterbeck and Middlebie, by a not very good road in any part,
and I noticed when we got into Ecclefechan
the school-house clock stood at twenty minutes to two. There were a great number of
people at the funeral in gigs and on foot, a
good number from Ecclefechan had gone
about a mile out towards Middlebie to meet.
It was a cloudy sunny morning with great
black clouds which threatened rain all day
although there was not any, and the sun's
rays came darting through a greyish mist in
long streaks of light which threw into relief
Repentance Hill, Woodcockaigne, and the si-
lent-looking steeples and roofs of Ecclefechan
itself, in a strange way. As I arrived at
Ecclefechan by the train from Dumfries
which reached there shortly after ten without
finding anyone else going there on the same
sad errand, I walked by the Common and
avoided the Main Street and so on to the
Kirkyard.

At the funeral there were few, even among
the goodly sprinkling of older men, whom I

knew either by sight or by name, and who were of the older generation. A number of the younger ones I knew, or could guess the names of, as people once around about Scotsbrig and Middlebie. One notable figure called "Auld John Kennedy, the Post," was pointed out to John Carlyle for some recognition as having been at school with Uncle James. A queer looking little man of small bulk and stature, and with a pair of small restless eyes which under the excitement of the moment appeared as if they might loup out of his head. I should think he must have been on the borders of ninety years of age by his appearance. The all absorbed interest and the earnestness of the old man's gaze into the proceedings as he held both his withered hands clenched to the top of the iron railings, was as impressive as it was wae and touching to look upon. So soon as he might — John Carlyle went to shake hands with him, and I did so too. So soon as the funeral was over I instantly took leave and found a relief in walking from Ecclefechan all the way to Lockerbie, rather than wait about for hours for a suitable train. I glanced at Main Hill in passing, but as there is an addition in the shape of a new dwelling house of red sandstone, and a couple of stories high, I was not certain about its identity at first, until I had it confirmed by after inquiry.

I hope you have been in as fair health as you could wish and I could sincerely wish, who have often thought of you and yours, to all of whom please offer my loving wishes. All here are well and would wish to send their love also.   Ever affectionately,

J. C. AITKEN.

I give here the conclusion of Mr. Reginald Blunt's account of the movement to preserve Carlyle's house : —

"The canvass was pushed vigorously forward from the beginning of 1895. Circulars and letters were widely distributed, the assistance of libraries throughout the country was invoked, and, by the invitation of the Lord Mayor, a crowded meeting was held at the Mansion House at the end of February, and addressed by Lord Ripon, the United States Ambassador, Mr. Leonard Courtney, Mr. Leslie Stephen, and Mr. Crockett. Funds came in slowly, but steadily ; auxiliary committees were formed in New York and in Glasgow, and over £400 was remitted from

America. By the end of April about £2000 had been collected, sufficient to complete the purchase, pay the expenses of the fund, and carry out part of the essential repairs. The freehold of the house was accordingly bought in May, and, after a careful survey of its actual condition, the necessary works were put in hand at the end of the month, and completed in June.

"The end of the season in London, and the occurrence of a General Election in July, rendered the arrangement of any opening ceremony impossible, and the House was therefore opened informally at the end of July, and was visited by over a thousand persons, from all parts of the world, during the next six weeks."

In December, 1897, at the age of eighty-four, died Janet Carlyle Hanning, the last surviving Carlyle of her generation. As the reader has seen, many of the foregoing letters were addressed to her. Those which had passed between other members of the family, and were afterward either carried by her beyond seas or sent to her in Canada, were preserved by Mrs. Hanning as precious memorials of family affection.

INDEX

The Riverside Press
CAMBRIDGE, MASSACHUSETTS, U. S. A.
ELECTROTYPED AND PRINTED BY
H. O. HOUGHTON AND CO.